'What are you so afraid of?' he asked, moving closer, dropping his other arm to the vehicle behind. 'Why is it so hard to make a decision?'

Sophie looked up at him, surprise at his sudden move turning her eyes wide, and shock at finding herself trapped neatly against the vehicle when she tried shuffling backwards filling them with alarm. 'Oh, nothing. I'd have to call the office. And change my flight booking, of course—although I don't know what time I'll be able to get away.'

She was babbling. Flustered again, and delightfully so. 'Is that all you're worried about?'

Her eyes darted from one side to the other, checking the positioning of his arms as if assessing her chances of escape.

Didn't she realise? It was much too late for escape.

Trish Morey is an Australian who's also spent time living and working in New Zealand and England. Now she's settled with her husband and four young daughters in a special part of South Australia, surrounded by orchards and bushland, and visited by the occasional koala and kangaroo. With a life-long love of reading, she penned her first book at the age of eleven, after which life, career, and a growing family kept her busy until once again she could indulge her desire to create characters and stories—this time in romance. Having her work published is a dream come true. Visit Trish at her website, www.trishmorey.com

Recent titles by the same author:

FORBIDDEN: THE SHEIKH'S VIRGIN*
HIS MISTRESS FOR A MILLION
THE RUTHLESS GREEK'S VIRGIN PRINCESS
FORCED WIFE, ROYAL LOVE-CHILD
THE ITALIAN BOSS'S MISTRESS OF REVENGE
THE SHEIKH'S CONVENIENT VIRGIN

*Part of the *Dark-Hearted Desert Men* mini-series

HIS PRISONER
IN PARADISE

BY
TRISH MOREY

™ MILLS & BOON®

First published in Great Britain 2010
Harlequin Mills & Boon Limited,
Eton House, 18-24 Paradise Road, Richmond, Surrey TW9 1SR

© Trish Morey 2010

ISBN: 978 0 263 87829 5

Harlequin Mills & Boon policy is to use papers that are natural, renewable and recyclable products and made from wood grown in sustainable forests. The logging and manufacturing process conform to the legal environmental regulations of the country of origin.

Printed and bound in Spain
by Litografia Rosés, S.A., Barcelona

HIS PRISONER
IN PARADISE

To editor extraordinaire, Jo Grant.

Thank you for your patience, your insight and
your wisdom, along with your wonderful advice
and support through these last 11 books!

Long may it continue.

With thanks, too,
to the generous and gracious Helen Bianchin.
A class act, an awesome writer,
and an inspiration in every way.

Thank you both!

CHAPTER ONE

'OVER my dead body!' Daniel Caruana hadn't made it past the first paragraph of his sister's email before he crumpled the printout in his fist and hurled it in fury at the closest wall. Monica marrying Jake Fletcher? No way in the world!

Not if he had anything to do with it!

Too wound up to sit, too agitated to stand still, he gave in to the need to pace, his long strides eating up length after length of his sprawling office's floor, while his restless hands took turns clawing though his hair. By his side, full-height windows took full advantage of the view of a white, sandy palm-lined beach and the azure sea that glinted under the tropical Far North Queensland sun.

Daniel saw nothing of it.

Daniel saw only red.

Whatever had possessed him to allow Monica to study in Brisbane? So far from Cairns, so far away from his influence. *And clearly nowhere near far enough away from the grasping hands of Jake Fletcher.*

He stopped pacing, his mind making connections that sent ice floes careening down his spine. Fletcher had called twice this week out of the blue, leaving messages for Daniel to call back, messages Daniel had brushed aside like he was swiping at an annoying insect needling at his skin. For he had no desire to speak to Fletcher ever again. Had no purpose.

But now it appeared Fletcher had purpose—if only to gloat…

Bile rose in his throat, its bitter taste the perfect accompaniment to his mindset. Please God, not Fletcher.

Please God, not his sister.

Especially after what had happened before.

Daniel leaned his forehead against the glass and closed his eyes, a vision remaining of a girl with laughing blue eyes and a sweet, sweet smile.

Emma.

As long as he drew breath, he would not forget Emma.

Nor what Jake Fletcher had done to her!

He opened his eyes and gazed far out to where the cerulean sea met the sky, searching for answers and solutions. Ordinarily the picture-postcard view was a sight that inspired him. Cheered him. Even, on occasion, soothed his fractured nerves.

Today all that sun-drenched perfection only served to mock the storm-tossed contents of his mind.

He slammed one palm against the glass. Damn—not Monica! He'd barely seen off Monica's last so-called boyfriend, an effort that had left him twenty-thousand dollars poorer on the deal. Small change, given what the jerk might have held out for if he'd done his homework a little more thoroughly and found out what his girlfriend was really worth.

Fletcher, on the other hand, probably knew how much the Caruana fortune was worth down to every last cent. Twenty-thousand dollars would be nowhere near enough to deter his kind, especially not now he probably imagined he was practically family.

No way. His fingers pressed hard against the glass, as rigid as his resolve. As long as Daniel had any say in it, Jake Fletcher would *never* be family.

Fletcher wouldn't come cheap—there was no doubt of that—but everyone had their price, and whatever it took to free Monica of his poison influence would be worth it.

The phone on his desk buzzed behind him. Daniel scowled at the interruption—surely his empire could cope for just ten minutes without him? Then he reached for it. After all, he hadn't taken the Caruana name from the brink of financial disaster to its dizzy heights by ignoring his businesses, whatever the reason.

He would deal with Fletcher—nothing was surer—but he would not lower his game in the process. His hand snatched up the receiver. 'What?'

A moment's hesitation met his retort, a moment in which he remembered it was a temp sitting outside and not his usual indestructible PA.

'Mr Caruana?' she squeaked. 'There's a Miss—a Miss Turner here to see you.'

His scowl deepened and for a second the problem of Fletcher took a back seat. He couldn't remember anything about any Miss Turner. 'Who?'

'Sophie Turner: from *One Perfect Day*.'

The name made no sense to him but he was used to people trying to talk their way into his office, looking for favours, or more frequently cash contributions towards shaky business-plans the banks had already turned down. This Miss Sophie Turner was no doubt another of their ilk. 'Never heard of her. Get rid of her.' He slammed the phone back down, annoyed again with the unnecessary interruption when he had important things on his mind.

Even more annoyed when the phone buzzed a second time not thirty seconds later. 'What is it this time?' he growled into the mouthpiece, unforgiving at the interruption, even if the girl didn't know better.

Her voice sounded even more timid. 'Miss Turner says it should have been in the email your sister sent you. All the details about her visit were apparently there.'

'What email?'

'You did read it?' the temp continued apologetically, a crack in her voice; she sounded as if any moment she would burst into tears. 'It was on your desk. I printed it out especially.'

That email? His eyes crossed to the crumpled ball of paper that had come to rest in a corner of the room. He hadn't got past the casual bombshell Moni had dropped that she intended to marry the one man he had reason to hate with a passion. How the hell was he expected to absorb anything more?

'Hold on,' he said, dropping the phone down on the desk and crossing the office floor in long, purposeful strides. He swept up the ball of paper and unscrewed it, flattening it against his broad palm. The paragraph stared out at him, the same one that had turned his vision red scant minutes before:

Daniel, please be excited for me. I thought I was sworn off men for ever, especially after being dumped for the third time in quick succession, but then I met Jake Fletcher and the last few weeks couldn't have been more perfect. He treats me like an absolute princess and he's asked me to be his wife, and I've said yes.

No; his mind revolted. *Never!* He closed his eyes, the same rush of anger winning supremacy over his veins, the same flood of revulsion as the first time. Little wonder he'd been unable to bring himself to read the rest. His fingers ached to crumple the page into a tight ball once more, but this time he took a deep breath, willed his eyes open and read on.

I know you two never used to get on in the past, and maybe that's why you didn't return Jake's calls last week, but I'm hoping you can put the past behind you when you see how much we love each other.

Put the past behind you? A thousand snapshots of a young woman's bright smile formed a moving slide-show through his consciousness. How was he ever supposed to put the past behind him when she would never get to see another day?

I know it's sudden but I want you to be among the first to know our happy news and just how much we love each other. It's the real thing this time, I know.

Daniel snorted his contempt. The real thing? He had no doubt Fletcher thought it the real thing, but if he was in love with anything it was the Caruana fortune. When would his sister ever learn that that was all men wanted? *Especially* men like Fletcher.

But she'd soon see the light, just as she had before, just as soon as he'd dispensed with this latest in a long line of gold-diggers whose so-called love didn't extend past her trust fund.

I wish I could give you this news personally, but you were in transit, and now Jake is whisking me off to Honolulu for two weeks for a surprise engagement present and there simply wasn't time to get a connection through Cairns to meet up before we left.

He growled, the fingers of his free hand curling and un-curling into a fist; bile wasn't the only bitter taste that filled his mouth. The thought of his little sister with *him* made him want to catch the next flight to Honolulu and drag her back before the bastard got her pregnant.

Or was that his intention— To make this marriage a done deal before the ceremony?

Daniel shook his head. It would take more than a baby before this marriage went ahead. The fires of hell would freeze over before he let someone like Fletcher marry his sister.

Monica was twenty-one now, so physically dragging her back was hardly an option, but there was no way he was going to stand by and let her get cornered into this marriage. Not by a long shot. He glanced down at the last few lines.

So instead I've arranged for our wedding planner to visit you. Her name is Sophie Turner and she's already much more than a friend. Will fill you in on the details later.
Meanwhile, be nice to her!

His sister had signed off with a promise to send a postcard from Waikiki Beach, but that wasn't what held his attention. It was the 'be nice to her'.

What did his sister take him for—some kind of monster?

He wasn't a monster. He was a businessman and a brother: a brother who had his eye out to protect his little sister from those who sought to take advantage of both her and the family fortune.

He was careful. Cautious. Protective of his own.

Did that make him such a monster?

Of course he'd see this Sophie Turner. And he'd be nice, just as his sister had requested. He'd invite her in, listen to her spiel and then he'd set her straight.

Because her services would not be required. As long as he drew breath, there would be no wedding between his sister and the likes of Jake Fletcher.

He picked up the receiver that lay abandoned on his office desk.

'Send Miss Turner in.'

CHAPTER TWO

SOPHIE perched uneasily on the edge of the waiting-room chair, the leather portfolio that contained all the details of Monica and Jake's wedding resting on her knees. She couldn't help but notice the bloom of pink spread over the young PA's cheeks as reluctantly she placed the second call to her boss in less than a minute. Clearly what she'd read on the Internet about Daniel Caruana's take-no-prisoners reputation extended beyond his business rivals and his girlfriends to his staff; the girl looked petrified.

Sophie might have felt guilty at insisting the girl call again and explain, but she wasn't about to waste an entire day travelling from Brisbane to Cairns and back again for no good reason—not when Monica had told her today's meeting had been all arranged and how much they were both relying on her.

'Oil on the waters', Jake had labelled her role, not exactly imbuing her with confidence. Apparently Daniel was super-protective of his little sister, having practically raised her since their parents had died, so of course he'd take the news of Monica's plans with less than enthusiasm. Especially given Jake and Daniel hadn't exactly hit if off back in high school, which Jake had admitted when attempting to explain why Daniel might not have bothered to answer his calls.

Something seriously wrong had gone on between them, Sophie mused, if Daniel wouldn't even speak to him. Her suggestion had been for Jake and Monica to visit Daniel themselves, given he could hardly refuse to see Jake if Monica was with him, but Monica had come up with what she thought was a more diplomatic solution.

She'd break the news to her brother in an email and then the to-be-weds would disappear for two weeks while Sophie ran through the wedding arrangements with Daniel. By the time the happy couple returned from Hawaii, Sophie would have everything arranged and Daniel would have come to terms with the idea that his little sister was a grown woman, old enough to make her own decisions about getting married and to whom.

It was simple, Monica had told her.

Failsafe.

Monica had hugged her tight and thanked her. She'd looked so hopeful, if not half-desperate, this bride-to-be who wanted everything to be absolutely perfect, Sophie had swallowed back all her arguments that it should be them visiting Daniel and ironing out any problems face to face, and had nodded her agreement instead.

Now it seemed a crazy idea. Conscious of time spinning away while the PA waited for a response, she clamped down on the bubble of nervousness that had her suddenly fidgeting with the folder perched on her knees.

Failsafe? She wished she could be so sure. Anyone who could put the fear of God into his receptionist with just a word or two was hardly likely to be the pushover Monica imagined her brother to be. But she supposed she had to meet the man some time, especially given they were practically related.

How ironic. She'd always wanted family; reconnecting with Jake after all their years apart had been amazing, even if it had taken their mother's death to get the siblings back together. Now it looked like her tiny family was set to expand. Monica was a sweetheart. The two of them had hit it off from the first time they'd met, and she couldn't imagine a nicer sister-in-law.

But somehow the prospect of being Daniel's sister-in-law didn't come with quite the same thrill. That was the down side of families, she supposed: you didn't always get to choose your relatives.

What was taking the man so long? Impatiently she crossed and uncrossed her ankles, unclipping the portfolio to check its contents were all present and correct before snapping it shut without having registered a thing. Damn the man and his arrogance! If he'd just bothered to talk to her brother, she wouldn't have to be here at all.

The girl shrugged apologetically at Sophie's questioning glance, and Sophie sighed and turned her attention out of the full-length windows to where the palm-fringed, sandy shore met the Coral Sea. Some PA's office, she thought. It was a million times better than her own office in Brisbane which boasted not even a sniff of river view between the multi-storey office blocks. Maybe there were compensations for working for the boss from hell. At least his PA had a decent view between the no-doubt frequent ear-bashings.

'Mr Caruana will see you now.'

Sophie jumped, her insides lurching at the announcement, and not entirely with relief. Sure, she'd got what she'd come here for—admittance to the hallowed inner sanctum for an audience with Mr High and Mighty—but there was no sudden burst of enthusiasm at the prospect. The time he'd taken to make up his mind was hardly welcoming, and if it was up to her she'd like nothing better than to turn and snub one Daniel Caruana's churlish and clearly reluctant agreement.

But this wasn't about her. She was here to champion Jake and Monica, and telling the man where to get off was hardly going to help. So instead she took a deep breath and smoothed the silk of her skirt as she rose, doing a last-minute check of her sheer stockings for ladders, and putting a hand to the sleek coil behind her head for any escaping tendrils.

Cool, poised and professional was the look and manner she was aiming for. The Daniel Caruana she'd researched demanded first-class presentation and she intended to deliver. Later, in the afterglow of a successful wedding between their respective siblings, and when they knew each other better, there would be time to relax in each other's company.

Because, while the prospect seemed unlikely at the moment, it would be nice if she could at least like the man who was soon to be her brother-in-law.

Though given what she'd experienced so far of Daniel Caruana, she wasn't too confident.

She smiled her thanks to the PA, whose colour had returned and who managed to smile back, clearly relieved she wasn't going to have to ring her boss a third time. Sophie rapped her knuckles lightly on the door and let herself into the largest office she'd ever seen.

She stopped dead, stunned by the sheer dimensions of the room. All this space for one man? *Maybe he needed it to accommodate his ego.* She shoved her scorn back where it belonged. He *had* agreed to see her, even if it had taken an eternity; maybe the man wasn't completely beyond redemption.

She worked up a smile, remembering the old adage that to think positive was to be positive. 'Mr Caruana,' she offered with an enthusiasm she didn't feel and that barely cloaked her nerves. 'It's a pleasure to meet you at last.'

He was standing with his back to her against the wall of windows that brought the best of the far-north Queensland beach views into the office, his arms crossed and feet planted wide apart. Maybe it was because she'd already witnessed the view that five storeys could offer over the coast line that Sophie found herself assailed with impressions that had nothing to do with the view outside and had no place on today's agenda.

Broad shoulders.

Narrow hips.

Long, lean legs.

Then he turned and the view outside faded to grey. She blinked, wondering what it was exactly that the pictures on the Internet had missed. Sure, they might have captured the short, tousled black hair, the steel-like gaze and the wide, generous lips. They might have contained a hint of the aura that surrounded him of power and success and raw masculinity. Yet they'd been unable to capture that grace of moment, that animal-like quality that turned even his slightest movement predatory.

His head tilted and his narrowed gaze assessed her, as if he had stripped through all her professional-development bluff and seen her for the nervous sister of the groom anxious to make a good impression that she really was. 'Is it a pleasure?'

Maybe not. Not that he was waiting for her answer. She got the distinct impression Daniel Caruana wasn't used to waiting for anything, even before he continued, 'You wanted to see me?'

'Ah.' She swallowed, his prompt reminding her why she was here, and that it wasn't to ogle the brother of the bride or lose herself in her thoughts. 'Of course.' She forced her frozen legs into motion and crossed the space between them, holding out her hand. 'Sophie Turner, from One Perfect Day. One Perfect Day makes perfect memories to last a lifetime.' The business's advertising blurb rattled off her tongue before she could stop herself. She was proud of her business and all she'd achieved. She believed that she offered her clients as perfect a wedding day possible, but right now in this office, faced with this man and battling her own rattled thought-processes, her words sounded trite and hackneyed.

He surveyed her hand for what felt like an eternity before his eyes once again lifted to snag on hers. This close she could see the dark shadow of a beard accentuating the strong line of his jaw. This close his dark eyes seemed to swirl with un-plumbed depths, the hint of a smile in those ever-so-slightly-upturned lips.

Then he finally took her hand in his and sent a jolt to her internal thermostat. She dragged in much-needed oxygen, only to find it fuelled with the warm, spiced tang of male. She pressed on, trying to ignore the feel of her hand in his, trying to discount the skin-on-skin contact and the scramble it was making of her senses. 'Monica has told me a lot about you. She wishes she could have visited you herself, to tell you about her plans, but—'

'But she was suddenly whisked away to Hawaii?' His voice was deep and rich and with the merest trace of an accent. It rolled over her senses much like the way his thumb seemed to be skimming the back of her hand. 'By the latest man she's apparently fallen head over heels in love with?'

The tension hummed through his words, an obvious cyni-cism shining in the gleam of his dark-as-night eyes, despite the easy smile that revealed a line of perfect white teeth.

That man, she wanted to say, *is my brother, and he loves Monica as much as she loves him.* But right now all her thoughts and senses were centred on the hand that somehow still remained firmly lodged within his.

Power, she felt in his touch, and a heat that radiated up her arm to fan out to her extremities in a delicious wave.

She tugged her hand free, sensing a slight reluctance on his part to let her go, and then wondered if she'd just imagined it.

Wished it were so.

Now she really was losing it.

Her eyes scanned the spacious office and fell on a nearby suite, three leather settees arranged in a U formation around a glass-topped coffee table. She sensed an opportunity to escape his close proximity and gather her scattered thoughts to the deal. 'Perhaps we could sit there?' she suggested with wash-day brightness laid on thick. 'And I can fill you in on Monica and Jake's plans.'

She was already seated, her briefcase beside her on the floor and unclipping her portfolio, when she realised he was still standing there, his lips curled again, a facsimile of a smile fading before reaching his eyes.

Then he seemed to shrug, making even that slight gesture look elegant and full of animal grace. 'Perhaps we could,' he agreed, before surprising her completely by ignoring the other sofas and sitting down alongside her, as if determined to turn her escape into purgatory.

He liked the way she seemed to shrink back against her armrest after that initial look of shock, especially after he'd angled himself sideways, snaking one arm along the back of the chair. Now she squeezed herself into the corner of the sofa and focused on sorting through the contents of the folder on her knees like it was some kind of lifeline. 'I have some brochures,' she mumbled, her long fingers fumbling.

She was flustered.

He liked a woman flustered. It kept her on the defensive, right where he wanted her. Unless she was in bed, of course, and there he welcomed the occasional tigress.

Would prim-looking Miss Turner be a tigress in bed?

He took his time to look at the woman alongside him up and down. The button-through blue silk dress with modest neckline hid more than it revealed, but first impressions had told him she had a reasonable body hidden beneath: nicely balanced in the hip and bust departments, slim-waisted and long-legged, with her facial features arranged just as acceptably as her body parts.

Second impressions only confirmed the first. Even in profile—the real test—her features were engaging. High cheekbones, a classic nose, that lush mouth…

He frowned. He couldn't remember the name, but something about her looked almost familiar. The thought was discarded the very next instant. He met a lot of women, and if he had met this one before he was sure he wouldn't have let her get away without knowing her better.

Unless she'd been out of bounds. Some people didn't share the same scruples, he knew from experience, but if there was one thing he wouldn't touch it was someone else's woman. 'Are you married, Miss Turner, or engaged?'

Her head snapped around, a couple of brochures sliding unnoticed from her fingers into her lap. 'Why do you ask?'

He smiled, scooping the pamphlets up, noticing with satisfaction the tremor as the back of his fingers skimmed the top of her legs; it was no more than a featherlight contact through the silk of her skirt, but enough to elicit the kind of reaction he was used to. The kind of reaction he welcomed when he himself was attracted. 'You work in the wedding business—wouldn't someone who has been married themselves understand what a bride really wants to make her day perfect? How else would you know?'

'Oh, I see, I…' Colour invaded her cheeks, and this time he kept his smile to himself. *Most definitely flustered.* Did she imagine he had ulterior motives in determining her marital status? Did she hope?

'It doesn't work that way,' she continued, accepting the brochures back and sweeping an imaginary strand of hair behind her ear, fiddling with an already perfectly aligned pearl earring. 'I've arranged more than one hundred weddings now. I can assure you, I've had plenty of experience to ensure Monica's wedding goes off without a hitch. Now—'

'So you're not married, then?'

She blinked, the shutters coming down over deep violet-coloured eyes, a movement that only drew attention to the long sweep of her dark lashes over the biggest surprise— cheeks flushed with sudden colour—before she once again opened them. Did she have any idea how innocent yet sexy she looked when she did that? He sighed. *What a waste.* In other circumstances he might have been able to pursue this attraction to its logical conclusion—in other circumstances he most likely would have. But she'd hardly be in the mood for sex once he'd given her the bad news.

'Did I say I wasn't married?'

'You intimated it, I'm certain.'

Her teeth pestered her bottom lip as she frowned, and he could tell she was rewinding her words, working out which of them had given her away. Then she shook her head. 'And is it actually relevant?'

'Not really.' He smiled, knowing he had her right where he wanted her. 'I'm just a curious kind of guy.'

The fog of indecision cleared in her narrowing eyes. 'In which case, you're no doubt curious to hear about Monica and Jake's plans.'

Touché, he thought, awarding her a mental tick of approval for steering the conversation back to the wedding. Except that it was the one place he didn't particularly want to go. 'Actually, no. I'd rather talk about you.'

Even with her mouth open he couldn't fault her looks. A shame the game had to end here. 'Mr Caruana,' she recovered enough to say, 'I don't think—'

A knock at the door had them both turning to where the young PA stood, looking uncertain. 'I'm sorry to interrupt, Mr Caruana. Would you like me to bring in any tea or coffee?'

'No, thank you. Miss Turner was just leaving. Let my driver know to have the car out front.'

He stood as the girl nodded, withdrew and pulled the door closed behind her—unnecessarily, given his guest would soon be leaving, but something he could easily remedy. Meanwhile his visitor was looking more flustered than ever. 'But Mr Caruana, we've hardly begun. We haven't even discussed the date for the wedding.'

'Ah, there would be a reason for that.' He was already reaching for the handle, ready to swing open the door in preparation for her departure. If she was about to storm out, as he predicted, he'd hate her to have to break her stride on the way. 'That's actually because we don't need to.' He swung the door open and waited. 'It would simply be a waste of time. And in my business—as in yours, I expect—time is money.'

She shook her head where she stood, a slash of colour accenting each high cheekbone. 'This is your own sister's wedding we're talking about. Surely you want to support her on the most important day of her life?'

'Whatever do you take me for? Of course I would never be so callous. My sister, and her happiness, are of the utmost concern to me.'

'Then why are you not prepared to even talk about the arrangements for her wedding?'

'There's a very simple explanation for that, Miss Turner, an explanation that seems to have escaped your notice: you see, there's actually not going to *be* a wedding.'

CHAPTER THREE

No WEDDING? She'd learned through her research that Daniel
Caruana was regarded as one of Far North Queensland's most
ruthless business tycoons, known equally for his ability to
create millions as for his ability to blow any opposition away.
Likewise she'd been warned by Jake that Daniel Caruana
was super-protective of his little sister and that her suddenly
getting married mightn't sit easily with him.

Still, the sheer force of his reaction shocked her. It was
one thing to want the best for his sister—who wouldn't want
that?—but to deny this wedding would happen, to pretend
that it would go away if he so decreed, just beggared belief.

'Is that so?' she managed, determination stiffening her
spine as slowly she rose to her feet, swallowing back on a
more personal, more biting, retort. 'I suspect Monica and Jake
might have something to say about that.'

'And I suspect my sister will soon see sense, and this marriage rubbish will be nothing more than a distant memory. In
which case, I'm sorry to say, it appears your services will no
longer be required.'

From somewhere deep inside her she summoned a smile.
She hadn't wasted a day to come and not see him. Likewise
she hadn't wasted a day to come and be summarily dis-
missed—not without him hearing her out. 'Mr Caruana,' she
said, knowing instinctively that if she took a step towards the

open door she would be giving in to his heavy-handed tactics. Instead she stood right where she was, clutching the portfolio and the wedding arrangements it contained to her chest as if protecting her own child.

Right this minute the wedding of Jake and Monica *felt* like her baby. She'd put so much time and effort into making sure Monica had everything she wished for—palm trees, a romantic beach setting and, hopefully, a glorious sunset to accompany the reception. Finding a venue that could provide all that and could take a wedding at short notice had consumed one hundred per cent of her time lately, and if it hadn't been for a cancellation she wouldn't have a booking at all. If she didn't confirm tomorrow morning like she'd planned, she'd lose it; she'd be blowed if she'd do that because His Nibs didn't like the idea of his little sister getting married. 'If I might be so bold, I don't think Monica and Jake consider it "rubbish". They would no doubt both be offended you felt that way, as am I.'

He glanced at his watch, managing to look both impatient and bored in the same instant. 'Is that all you have to say before you leave?'

'No, as a matter of fact, it's not. For as much as you might be able to dismiss me from your office and continue living in your precious little world of denial, you're going to have to face the fact some time that your sister is all grown up now and she and Jake will soon be married, with or without your seal of approval—which I'm sure you appreciate, given Monica's age, she doesn't actually need.

'Naturally, I don't need to tell you that she'd be happier if you could dredge up some semblance of support for her at this, one of the most important times of her life, but the marriage is going to go ahead whether you like it or not. In which case, it might be better and easier for all concerned if you just accepted that fact now rather than fighting it, wouldn't you say?'

She wanted to sag with relief after completing her impromptu speech, but there was no respite, not from the steel-like glare that held her pinned to the spot, nor from the fury drawing his features into a tight mask.

Beyond the glass walls of the office the sun continued to blaze in an azure sky. The diamond-flecked waves along the shore were studded with swimmers taking advantage of the warm winter sun, while inside the temperature had dropped below freezing.

Suddenly the door slammed shut with a crash that made the walls shudder and Sophie jump with them as Daniel stormed away along the length of the windows. Just as suddenly he stopped and turned, his hand slashing through the air. 'I don't have to accept anything! Not when there will *be* no wedding!'

'You really think you can stop them?' She dragged in a breath, shaking her head, realising that arguing was futile and that she would do better to try and persuade. 'Look, Mr Caruana,' she said, taking a tentative and what she hoped was a conciliatory step forward, 'Monica and Jake are crazy about each other. You should see them together—this is a true love-match.'

His left palm cracked down so hard on his timber desk that she flinched. 'She does *not* love that man!'

'You don't know that.'

'Don't you think I know my sister? Monica likes to think she's in love. She always has. She's been in love with fairy tales for ever, in love with the *idea* of being in love, always waiting for a knight in shining armour to come riding over the hill and rescue her. But if there's one thing my sister doesn't need it's rescuing. Not by anyone.'

No? With a brother like him, rescuing by a knight in shining armour sounded like a perfectly reasonable idea, if not a necessity. 'I'm not actually talking fairy tales, Mr Caruana. I'm talking about love—deep, abiding love.' She hesitated, wondering how far she could go before overstepping the mark from 'cool and professional' to tripping into 'foot in mouth' territory. Then she figured that, with all that had gone before, she was already there. 'I gather from your reaction that you're unfamiliar with the concept.'

The sudden tightness of flesh against cheek and jaw was his first response. 'I'm talking reality!' was his second, before he took to pacing again, eating up the floor in long, fluid strides. She would have liked to ignore him, but she was compelled to watch. Compelled to admire the big-cat-like grace and economy of his movements, even when anger seemed to be the prime motivator behind his motion.

Whoever his tailor was, he was a genius, she thought guiltily; there was no way he'd bought those trousers off the rack. The fabric moved over the tight musculature of his behind and thighs like it was part of his very flesh.

'How much do you think my sister is worth?' He wheeled around so suddenly she had to drag her eyes north, and her wayward thoughts with them. 'How many millions?'

Sophie shrugged, struggling for nonchalance as she reined in thoughts that had no place in this confrontation. 'And that's relevant because?' It seemed a fair question to her—she'd never given two thoughts to Monica's wealth or otherwise—but it only appeared to make him madder.

'Are you really that naïve, Miss Turner?' Three long steps brought him closer—perilously closer. Now there was only a pace between them, and even that seemed shrunken and almost vibrating with tension, a tension that inexplicably made her breasts ache and her nipples harden. 'Do you have any idea how many men have come sniffing after my sister, hoping to find a way to the Caruana fortune?'

She forced herself to concentrate on his words instead of the shimmering sensations of the flesh, kicking up her chin in a futile effort to appear taller, even though he had at least six inches on her five-foot-eight frame. 'And you'd know that was their motive, because…?'

'Because as soon as they got a sniff of a cheque they conceded defeat and cleared off.'

Shimmer turned to shock, rendering her momentarily speechless. When she could finally put voice to thoughts again, out spilled the disbelief in words. 'You paid them?'

She put a hand over her mouth, swaying a little on her feet at the revelation. Monica had mentioned in passing the fact that she'd never been able to hang on to a boyfriend for long, how she'd been left cold on more than one occasion and how she felt Jake was different. Sophie had imagined it had merely been to do with not finding the right guy yet, and had never once imagined there was a more sinister reason. 'You actually *paid* your sister's boyfriends to back off?'

'Which they did. Which proves my point, wouldn't you say, that they only wanted her for the money?'

She was still reeling, amazed that he was so unabashed about his interference on the one hand, and imagining the pressure he must have exerted on his sister's hapless suitors on the other. Confronted by one of his henchmen, or worse still Daniel himself, they'd probably been terrified of what might have happened if they didn't take the money and run.

She searched his eyes for some hint of remorse but their dark depths were cold and unapologetic. She shivered, the earlier shimmering heat she'd felt suddenly vanquished with his cold-as-ice revelation.

She had no doubt he thought he was doing good in protecting the family fortune, but in doing so he'd left his sister thinking there was something fundamentally wrong with her and that she would never find a partner who would stick by her in the process.

It was sheer luck that Monica had found Jake—not that there was any way she was going to convince Daniel of that. Just as clearly she could tell she'd wasted her time coming here today. Daniel didn't just want his sister to remain unmarried, what he really wanted was to lock her in a gilded cage and throw away the key.

'You should be pleased your sister has found someone who appreciates how special she is.'

'Oh, Fletcher knows she's special, all right. Special to the tune of an eight-figure sum. Why else would he have zeroed in on her?'

'Because he loves her.'

'So why the desperate rush to marry if he *loves* her so much? Is he afraid she'll change her mind and he'll lose his entrée to a fortune? Or is it that he can't wait to get his hands on her assets—those assets he hasn't already availed himself of, that is?'

'You're disgusting,' she managed, already turning her thoughts to getting to the airport, maybe catching an earlier flight back to Brisbane. 'You're not a brother. You're some kind of monster.'

'Am I more a monster than the men who would take advantage of Monica's fortune in pretence of love?'

She bowed her head, disbelieving, already turning away. 'You don't know they were after her money. They were probably just too terrified to argue. I'm sorry, I've wasted—'

An iron grip on her forearm put a stop to her escape before it had begun. When she turned back, his eyes were narrowed, their darkness intensified, his head at an angle as he moved closer. 'Yet you're not too terrified to argue, are you, Miss Turner? Why is that? Are you afraid of missing out on your big, fat fee?'

Resistance sparked once more in her veins. 'Is that all everything comes down to with you, Mr Caruana? Money? Do you really believe everyone is motivated by the same almighty quest for the dollar? Well, maybe you should think again. And then maybe you might stop judging everyone by your own low standards.'

She jerked her elbow out of his grip, wanting to get away, needing to get away. Failure weighing heavily on her shoulders.

Oil on the waters. What a laugh. She might as well have thrown petrol on the flames of his familial discontent. She'd blown her role as peacemaker completely. 'I have to go.'

'Why? So you can warn Fletcher I'll be making him an offer? To advise him he should hang out for more? You mark my words,' Daniel continued, 'Fletcher will have his price, just like the rest.'

'Oh no.' She shook her head. There was no way Daniel was slotting her brother into the likes of his damned fortune-hunters. 'Jake isn't like that—even if those others were, and you've given me no proof of that. Jake isn't interested in her money. He loves Monica.'

'Of course he does,' he sneered. 'How long exactly have they known each other? A fortnight? A month?'

'Some people don't need that long to know the person they're with is the one they want to spend the rest of their lives with.'

'Is that so? Next you'll be telling me you believe in love at first sight.'

'It happens.'

'But of course you would have to say that, in your line of work. You want people to get married; you don't actually care if they *stay* married.'

Sophie turned for the door. 'Look, I'm leaving. I don't have to put up with this.'

But he was already there in front of her, blocking her exit, and again she was struck by the way he moved with such effortless grace for such a powerfully built man. But it was what he was doing to her internal thermostat that concerned her more. Again he'd tripped some switch that sent her body from frigid to simmering in an instant. Her skin prickled with heat, her nerve endings tingled with awareness and it was only the portfolio clutched in her folded arms that concealed her rock-hard nipples.

It was in his eyes, she realised as he stared down at her. In his dark, challenging eyes that could suddenly turn from cold and flat to molten pools that radiated their heat to hers and then downwards to her very extremities. Eyes that were telling her things that made no sense, yet still her toes curled in her shoes.

Then he smiled and reached out a hand, running the backs of his fingers down her cheek so gently that she trembled under his electric touch. It was like being in a bubble where the room had shrunk to a tiny space around them, where even her peripheral vision had shrunk to fit no more than his broad shoulders. 'If I said to you right now "marry me", would you say yes?'

His voice seemed to come from a long, long way away, while his thumb stroked her chin; her lips parted on a sigh. 'Mr Caruana…' She swallowed, her thoughts scrambled. She was supposed to be leaving. She was sure she'd been about to leave. They'd been arguing. But what about?

'Daniel,' he said, his voice like the darkest chocolate, smooth, rich and forbidden. 'Enough with the "Mr Caruana". Call me Daniel. And I shall call you Sophie.'

'Mr Caruana,' she attempted again. 'Daniel.' She licked her lips. The name felt way too informal, tasted almost intimate, or was that just the way his eyes seemed to spark and flare as he watched her mouth his name? As he watched her lips taste the sound as hungrily as she'd watched his lips utter her name?

He was closer, his hand at her neck, drawing her towards him, towards his mouth. 'What would your answer be?'

There was a point to all this, she recognised that much, if only she could tell what it was. But in air spiced with his musky, masculine scent she couldn't make sense of what he was asking, only on some fundamental level that it shouldn't be happening. She held onto the thread of logic, clung to it, even when his lips brushed over hers and then returned for another pass just as feather-light as the first. Just as earth shattering.

She trembled under the silken assault, her knees almost buckling beneath her as he drew her closer until her folded arms met his chest, the folded arms protecting the folder she clung to like a shield, reminding her why she was here.

And it wasn't to allow herself to be seduced by the man who opposed his sister's marriage! She freed one hand and pushed against the hard wall of his chest, trying not to think about how good his hard flesh felt under her fingers even as the fingers deep in her hair attempted to steer her still closer.

Sophie turned her head aside, felt the brush of his warm breath on her cheek this time. 'Mr Caruana,' she pleaded, needing the formality to put distance between them. 'This is ridiculous. We barely know each other.'

His hands were gone from her as he wheeled away and cold air rushed to fill the places he'd been. 'Exactly my point,' he said, sounding angry, his back to her as he gazed out at the view, raking the fingers of both hands through his hair. 'We hardly know each other. And yet you seem to think it's perfectly reasonable for my sister to marry someone she's known barely a month.'

'So maybe Jake didn't maul her the first time they met.'

His shoulders stiffened before he turned and already she regretted her hasty words, even before she'd seen the potent depths of his eyes. 'Believe me, if I'd have mauled you I would have left the marks to prove it.'

A quake shuddered through her bones and she had to muster every last crumb of control she could to hide it. He'd touched her with a caress as soft as silk, and that had been enough to leave its mark, so how much more delicious would it be to feel the full brunt of his passion?

Oh yes, she believed him. Which was why now, more than ever, she had to get out of here. She was supposed to be a professional wedding planner, and professionals didn't get involved with family members of people whose weddings they were arranging, even when the groom was your brother. *Especially* when the groom was your brother. 'Like I said, I have to go.'

Yes; the sooner she went, the better. Her colour was high, her hair was mussed where he'd pushed his fingers in the thick coil and her eyes were wide and watchful, like she was afraid he'd kiss her again. The chances were, if she kept looking at him that way, he just might.

Why had he done that? He'd wanted to prove a point, to make her see how ridiculous it was for anyone to make the momentous step of getting married when they barely knew each other. Instead he'd got lost somewhere along the line, somewhere between the sensual curve of her cheek and the warm scent of woman.

'The car's waiting downstairs to take you to the airport.'

She nodded, leaning to gather her portfolio and briefcase without taking her eyes from him, as if to check he wasn't about to ambush her again. Then she straightened and headed for the door.

Halfway there, she stopped and turned. 'I feel sorry for you—I really do. But I feel sorrier for Monica, who thinks the sun shines out of her big brother. Who believes you love her and that you'll come round to her plans for marriage, when all you're really interested in is keeping her locked away from the world in some kind of gilded cage.'

'I want what's best for her.'

'No, you don't. You want what's best for *you*. What's easiest. You actually don't care about Monica's happiness at all. Well, all I can say is it's lucky she found someone like Jake at last, someone with a bit of backbone who can stand up to her overbearing, bullying brother. God knows, he'll need it.'

Her words rubbed him raw, her arguments playing on his mind. Once again she was defending the indefensible. Once again she was acting as if Fletcher were the injured party in all this. Fletcher was supposed to be her client but, the way she came out fighting every time he mentioned his name, anyone would think she was in love with him herself.

She was already reaching for the door handle when he found the words to respond. 'You don't know the first thing about Fletcher. Why do you insist on defending him the way you do?'

Her hand stilled on the handle. He saw her shoulders rise and fall on a sigh before she glanced over at him even as she pulled open the door. 'Why wouldn't I defend Jake? After all, he is my brother.'

CHAPTER FOUR

FLETCHER was her brother? She'd pulled the door closed behind her and disappeared before he could react, but it was shock that kept him rooted to the spot. Fletcher didn't have any sister, not that he could recall. He'd certainly never mentioned one in all their years at college, not that they'd ever spent any time in idle chit-chat. Daniel had always been too busy facing up to the brash challenger who'd insisted he was as good, if not better, than him, Fletcher trying to prove it at every opportunity. Besides, she'd said her name was Turner— or was that just part of the ruse?

Nothing made sense.

Nothing but knowing that he should have handled the meeting with her a whole lot better. He would have, if he hadn't been thrown off balance completely this morning by his sister's email.

And now the mess he'd made of the meeting had grown a hundred times worse. Because Sophie Turner wasn't simply a wedding planner, as he'd believed. She was Fletcher's sister.

She should have told him. He glanced out of the windows in the direction of the street, caught a glimpse of the car as it pulled into the traffic before it was lost from view and swore under his breath.

But of course she hadn't told him. She was probably in on the deal, no wedding planner at all but rather a convenient intermediary, no doubt expecting a cut for her part in playing a role and making the marriage plans look real. She'd probably be calling Fletcher already, telling him to expect an offer, advising him to hang out for a better one.

Or would Monica and Fletcher still be on their flight?

Maybe there was still time.

He snatched up the phone on his desk and punched in a number that would connect him with his head of security. It answered on the second ring, as he knew it would. 'Jo? Caruana here. I want you to find out all you can about a wedding-planning business called One Perfect Day, and a Miss Sophie Turner who supposedly works there. I want financials, personal contacts and history, as well as details of family members of every employee, as fast as you can.'

'Will do,' came the rapid-fire response. Then a pause. 'Do I take it congratulations are in order?'

From anyone else the question would not have been tolerated, but Jo had been with him almost from the beginning, their association going back to their high-school days together.

'I'm not. But Jake Fletcher's apparently got his hooks into Monica. They're talking weddings, and Sophie Turner claims to be their wedding planner.'

'Fletcher's back?' Daniel heard the squeak of his security head's chair as he sat to attention. 'You want me to sort him out, boss?'

Daniel had anticipated just such a reaction. Jo hated Fletcher almost as much as Daniel himself did. But then Jo was the one who'd been waiting at the airport when Daniel had returned from Italy in time for Emma's funeral. He was the one who'd kept him together when they'd learned the results of the autopsy. And he was the one who'd stopped him marching into Fletcher's hospital ward and pulling him off his life support.

He appreciated the loyalty, but while once upon a time he'd have settled contests with his fists, those days were gone. These days he preferred to use subtler, even if more expensive, means. Not that he couldn't afford it.

'He's already flown the coop and taken Monica to Hawaii—and left the wedding planner to convince me the wedding's kosher, no doubt to secure a higher settlement.'

'Like hell it's kosher! Okay, boss, I'm onto it.'

'And Jo—something else you should know.'

'What's that?'

'The wedding planner, Sophie Turner, she's claiming to be Fletcher's sister.'

Jo whistled through his teeth. 'I never knew Fletcher had a sister.'

'Neither did I. That's one of the things I want you to check. If she's not his sister, she's probably in on some kind of percentage from a settlement to make him disappear. And if she is his sister…'

'Given her scum dog of a brother, she'd be even less trustworthy.'

'Exactly what I was thinking,' Daniel agreed before he hung up, still leaning over his desk, hauling air into his lungs as his brain made the connections. Fletcher had to have taken Monica to Hawaii for two reasons—first, to ensure nobody could arrive in Brisbane while Fletcher wasn't around and bundle her on the next flight back to Cairns to talk her out of making the biggest mistake of her life, and secondly to suck her further and further into his web.

Meanwhile the sweet Miss Turner had the job of playing the supporting role at home to make it look like the wedding was real, no doubt in the hope it would crank up any pay-off offered to Fletcher.

He growled. If she'd been speaking the truth, then he'd had Fletcher's sister right here in his office and he'd let her walk away. God, he'd even held her in his arms and all but kissed her. Fletcher's damned sister. What had he been thinking?

But he hadn't been thinking then, not beyond the silky-smooth perfection of her skin, the unusual blue of her eyes, and the tantalising scent of woman.

So much for wanting to make a point about the irrationality of things happening too quickly. If she hadn't stopped him, if she hadn't pushed him away, he doubted he could have stopped himself.

Not the point he'd been trying to make at all. But Monica's news had thrown him for six. No wonder he hadn't been thinking straight.

But he was thinking straight now.

The old and familiar competitiveness cranked back into life. Fletcher would soon be sitting in his five-star hotel suite waiting to hear from his sister about Daniel's reaction, rubbing his hands together in glee while he waited for a nice plump offer for him to disappear to drop into his lap.

The last thing he'd be expecting would be for Daniel to join in the game. If Fletcher wanted to play 'whisk away the sister', why couldn't Daniel do likewise?

Maybe he should just *whisk away* one Miss Sophie Turner for however long it took.

And he sure as hell wouldn't let her go again until he knew Moni was safe.

He glanced at his watch. They should be nearing the airport by now. Miss Turner would be thinking she was just about home free.

He picked up the telephone again, punching in another number and smiling for what felt like the first time today, already anticipating her confusion. 'Cedric, there's been a change of plans…'

Sophie pushed back into the butter-soft upholstery, willing herself to relax. She'd almost turned her back on the car waiting for her when she'd emerged from the lobby. She'd had enough of Daniel Caruana for one day, and she'd wanted nothing more to do with him and his. But the driver had greeted her with a friendly smile and, much as she resented his boss, she'd had no reason to be rude to an innocent driver—especially one who was probably smiling in relief because it wasn't Mr Arrogance himself that he was picking up. Besides, she'd had no idea how long it would take to wait for a taxi this far north of Cairns, and the sooner she made it to the airport, the better chance she would have of catching an earlier flight back to Brisbane.

So she'd allowed herself to be handed into the spacious interior of the luxury sedan, satisfied at least that every minute took her another kilometre from Daniel Caruana.

She sighed and dropped her head back against the head rest, closing her eyes and wondering what she was going to tell Jake and Monica. They'd expected resistance to the wedding news, certainly, but Daniel hadn't even given her a chance to explain the wedding arrangements and the fact that nobody was expecting him to pay for anything. Not that he would have believed her, given he'd already made his mind up on that point.

Apparently nobody went out with his sister unless they were gold-digging fortune-hunters looking for nothing more than a juicy pay-out. And of course he wouldn't care who was supposed to stump up for the wedding bills. Hadn't he already made it plain that there was to *be* no wedding?

Sophie put a hand to her forehead, her fingers trying to stroke away her tension as the car continued down the palm-lined highway towards the city of Cairns and the airport that promised escape. How on earth had Jake ever thought she'd be able to convince someone like Daniel Caruana that this wedding was a good idea? And how was she going to tell him that she'd blown her peace-keeping role big time?

She opened her eyes in time to see the sign signalling the turn off for James Cook Airport. She sighed in relief. At least she'd soon be away from here. Away from Daniel Caruana, the man who could be her brother-in-law.

The man who had almost kissed her…

She jammed her eyes shut, trying to blot away the memories, but she could still feel the brush of his lips, could still smell his intoxicating, masculine scent weaving its way into her senses as his fingers worked their way into her hair and directed her face towards his.

When he'd told her that if he had mauled her she'd have the marks to prove it… Oh my. Sophie dragged in a lungful of air, hot and breathless, the car's air conditioning was suddenly found wanting. Thank goodness she'd found the sense to turn away before she made more of a fool of herself than she already had.

What was his point? Had he been trying to convince her he was the red-hot lover the tabloids hinted at? Or had he just been toying with her, like some random plaything, before throwing her out?

Either way, the man clearly had no conscience. She was glad she'd have nothing more to do with him. At least not until the wedding—if he even bothered to show up.

Then she smiled. If there had been one glimmer of satisfaction she could take from this morning's meeting, it had been the moment before she'd left, when she'd finally had the opportunity to tell him she was Jake's sister. In the scant seconds after her revelation, and before she'd pulled the door closed behind her, she'd seen his look of smug dismissal give way to shock and a kind of numb disbelief.

So maybe she hadn't managed to convince Mr Hot Shot Caruana to give his blessing to his sister's upcoming wedding—and maybe she'd blown her role as peace maker—but at least she'd managed to get the last word in. How fortunate it was that he hadn't allowed her to get a word in edgeways so she could save that little gem until last. That part of the meeting, at least, had been infinitely satisfying.

Sophie looked up, thinking for a moment that the driver had said something to her, only to find him talking into his hands-free phone. She looked around. They were in the departure lane, slowing as they neared the drop-off zone with the maze of vehicles pulling in and out along the kerb before them. She strung her briefcase strap over her shoulder, her hand ready on the door release so that she could quickly alight. Except the driver didn't pull in to stop like she'd expected but kept on driving.

'There's a spot just there,' she called, pointing to her left, wondering what was wrong with the last two spaces he'd driven past.

'Sorry, miss,' the driver said, glancing at her in his rear-view mirror. 'Change of plans.'

'No, I have a flight to catch.' She looked over her shoulder as the airport buildings and her escape plans disappeared behind, the first frisson of fear slipping down her spine and taking root in her gut.

She turned back in time to catch the driver's shrug as he accelerated back along the airport exit-road. 'Didn't Mr Caruana tell you? Apparently now you're going by chopper.'

'What? No.' Fear turned to anger as she reached for her PDA and found his number. 'No, Mr Caruana didn't tell me that.'

Mr Caruana still wasn't telling her anything. The young PA told her he was unavailable and couldn't be reached—perhaps she'd like to leave a message?

No, Sophie decided, breaking the connection. What she had to say to Mr Caruana was best said face to face. No matter what stunt he was pulling now, she'd make sure there'd be ample opportunity for that sometime.

She called her office in Brisbane, something she'd been intending to do once she'd confirmed her flight.

'Meg,' she said as soon as her assistant answered. 'It's Sophie.'

'How did the meeting go?'

Sophie pulled a face. 'Not as well as it could have. I think Monica might be walking down the aisle by herself.'

'Oh, I'm sorry to hear that. But at least you tried. What time will you be back?'

Good question, Sophie thought, biting her lip as she watched the passing parade of palm trees lining the wide highway, heading the wrong way, wondering if she should let Meg know what was happening. But what *was* happening? It wasn't like she was being kidnapped. Not exactly. She still had her phone, after all. It wasn't as if she couldn't call for help if she thought she needed it. But that still didn't mean she was happy about her plans being turned upside down for no good reason and without explanation. 'I'm not sure,' she said, and at least that much was true. 'It looks like I might be delayed. I'll let you know as soon as I can.'

'Okay. I'll hold the fort until you get back. Oh, and don't forget, you have that meeting at the Tropical Palms first thing tomorrow to finalise the arrangements.'

'Don't worry, Meg.' Whatever surprises Daniel Caruana had planned, she'd be back in Brisbane long before then. 'There's no way I'd miss that. See you soon.'

She snapped her phone shut and looked around. Here the rainforest covered mountains rose sharply from the narrowing coastal plain, and she realised she was almost back at the Palm Cove turn off and the office she'd left barely forty minutes ago. What the hell was he playing at? Surely he didn't feel so bad about the way he'd behaved during their meeting that he was going to make up for it by having her flown all the way to Brisbane in his private helicopter? She swallowed. As much as she wanted to get back to the office, she wasn't sure she was too crazy at the idea of spending two hours or so in one of those tiny buzz boxes.

But no, she decided, a man like Daniel Caruana wouldn't do remorse. It wouldn't be in his vocabulary. So what was he trying to prove?

Anxiety warred with anger inside her. Her stomach felt like it was already taking flight. The thought of going into battle with the man again set her nerves jangling, and her senses to high alert, but if he wanted a battle that was exactly what he would get.

Because, whoever Daniel Caruana thought he was, however much money he had, he had no right to ride roughshod over other people's wishes and plans. Not his sister's. Not her brother's. And least of all hers. She was just in the mood to explain that to him.

They turned off the highway, the car pulling into a clearing not far from the office block where a sleek red helicopter sat amidst a circle of white markers, its rotors lazily circling. But it was the tall, dark haired figure standing alongside a black coupe that was even sexier looking than the chopper that Sophie focused on. He was holding a phone to his ear, the other hand in his trouser pocket as he leaned against the low sports car, his long legs crossed casually at the ankle, his white open-necked shirt rippling softly in the breeze. He looked relaxed, urbane and totally without a hint of apology, which only made Sophie even more angry.

She was out of her door and on her way across to him before the car had barely stopped. He saw her coming, and even behind his sunglasses she could feel his dark eyes following her every step. But she was damned if she was going to let that slow sizzle under her skin bother her, not when it gave her yet another reason to resent him.

She stopped directly in front of him, although that still left her more than a metre away, courtesy of the long legs so idly stretched out in front of him. 'Do you mind telling me what this is about? I've got a flight back to Brisbane to catch, and the last thing I need is to be brought back here without one word of explanation.'

He uttered something into his phone and slid it shut, deposited it in the top pocket of his shirt and slipped that hand into his free trouser pocket. He looked so brutally good-looking and so frustratingly unmoved that she felt like tearing him limb from limb, if only to get a reaction. 'Miss Turner,' he said with a smile a crocodile would have been proud of, a smile that irritated her all the way down to her bones. 'I'm so pleased you could join me.'

'You've got a nerve. You know I had no choice.'

'Did Cedric tie you up and throw you in the boot?' His eyebrows rose. 'I must speak to him about his technique. I've warned him about treating my guests that way.' He gave a nod to someone over her shoulder, and she turned to see the driver give an answering wave as he drove off. She swung back, her indignation turning to fury.

'You think this is funny?'

'I think your reaction is slightly amusing, yes.'

The blood in her veins simmered and spat. 'Because I object to having my plans to return to Brisbane thrown into disarray by a man who made it plain my presence wasn't welcome here? You have a strange sense of humour, Mr Caruana.' She threw a glance at the chopper. 'Is that thing waiting to take me to Brisbane?'

'That's not exactly what I had in mind, no.'

'Then you can just forget whatever you had in mind. I'll do what I should have done before and call myself a taxi.' She wheeled away, pulling her phone from her bag, but she'd barely slid it open when it was extracted smoothly from her hands.

Something inside her snapped. She spun around, lunging for his hand. 'You bastard! Give that back.'

'Such language. I should have picked you for Fletcher's sister from the start.'

Her open palm cracked against his cheek so hard that her hand stung with fire at the impact, and she fervently hoped his cheek hurt at least half as bad. 'Did you bring me back merely so you could further insult my family?'

Open-jawed, he rubbed one side of his face where the darkening bloom was already spreading under his olive skin. 'Miss Turner,' he said, looking down at her, crowding her with an almost feral gleam in his eyes. It was with some satisfaction that she saw that any hint of a smile had been wiped from his face. 'You continue to surprise me.'

'I'm sorry I can't return the compliment. I was warned to expect an arrogant bastard used to throwing his weight around. Seems like I heard right. And now—' she held her hand out to him '—may I have my phone back? I have a plane to catch.'

His fingers only seemed to curl tighter around the device. 'What time is your flight?'

'What's it to you?'

'Because where I want to take you is only ten minutes away.'

'Why should I agree to go anywhere with you?'

'Would it help if I said I didn't give you a fair hearing during our meeting today?'

She was more suspicious than ever now. 'I think we both know that's true, but you didn't have to drag me back here to admit it. You could have called. I do have a phone…' She stared pointedly at the fingers still curled around her mobile. 'Or, at least, I did.'

He chose to ignore her reminder. 'It occurred to me after you left that I can't stop my sister getting married if that's what she really wants.'

'That's not what you said before.'

'Hear me out. I take it Monica would actually like me to be at her wedding?'

Sophie bristled. She'd been thinking that a wedding without a certain Daniel Caruana in attendance held a considerable appeal. But he was Monica's brother, and getting Daniel's cooperation was the reason she'd been sent up here. So she nodded reluctantly, little more than a tiny dip of her head in acknowledgement. 'Monica was hoping you might walk her down the aisle. When I left your office, that prospect didn't look too likely.'

'You haven't told her?'

She shook her head. 'Not yet. They'll still be *en route*.'

He looked skywards, exhaling as if relieved, one hand raking through his thick black hair. Sophie's eyes were involuntarily drawn to the broad expanse of chest, the uninterrupted view of his strong neck and the deep-olive skin revealed by his open-necked shirt. Monica was tiny when compared to her brother. Her skin was almost a honey gold whereas Daniel's was burnished bronze, as if he spent as much time as he could with his shirt off, soaking up the rays. She swallowed. She really didn't need to think about Daniel Caruana undressed. *Not one bit.*

She blinked, mentally chasing the unwanted thoughts away, only to find him watching her, a glimmer of something predatory in his dark eyes that disappeared even before she'd turned her eyes away, feigning interest in the fringe of palms bordering the lot. Heat flooded to her face. God, he'd seen her ogling him like some drooling teenager—a man she couldn't even stand. She'd clearly been in the Far North Queensland sun far too long.

'I'm sorry,' he said beside her.

Not as sorry as I am, she thought before his words sank in and she realised he was talking about something else entirely.

'You are?' It was the last thing she'd expected from him.

Her reaction brought a smile to his face. 'I'm not in the habit of apologising,' he told her. 'It does not come easily to me.' He sighed and looked over at the waiting helicopter and held up his hand to the pilot, his fingers splayed. The pilot nodded and turned away.

'Walk with me a while,' Daniel said beside her, strolling off towards the trees and a flower bed bursting with colour. 'Let me explain. You see, my sister's—Monica's—email took me by surprise. I hadn't had time to assimilate her news before you arrived on my doorstep. But you were right. She has never seemed so serious about any man, but she is twenty-one and I can't stop her getting married, if that's what she really wants.'

'It is what she wants.'

He paused, looking as though he was searching for acceptance, although the tic in his jaw looked anything but accepting. 'And if that is indeed so, then I should at least give you a fair hearing, if only for my sister's sake.'

They wandered closer to the flower bed where it seemed colour was king. Every colour seemed vivid here, she mused, the reds more vibrant, the greens more intense, oranges looking like flames from the fires of hell. Nothing, it seemed, was pastel, least of all the man walking alongside her right now. He was large and powerful and darker in impression than any man had a right to be, and it wasn't just the flowers that looked like they'd stepped straight from hell. With his chiselled dark beauty and the power he wore like a cloak, he could be the ruler of the underworld.

She stopped and shivered slightly, not liking the direction of her thoughts, turning instead towards the waiting chopper, the pilot sitting patiently at the controls. 'So why the chopper?'

'Where is the wedding to be held?'

She groaned inwardly. Couldn't he just answer a simple question? The man was jumping around so much it was impossible to get a handle on him. He'd gone from arrogant to abusive to underhand to reconciliatory in the time most people could have lingered over a lazy Sunday brunch. But, then again, what did his character faults really matter as long as he did right by his sister and her brother? It wasn't as though Sophie had to like him. Not that there was any chance of that.

'I've booked the Tropical Palms golf club on the Gold Coast. I'm confirming it tomorrow, first thing.'

He scowled, and if his PA had been here, Sophie could imagine the girl running for cover. 'A *golf club* is going to play host to my sister's wedding?'

She wasn't his PA and yet still she bristled, feeling defensive, knowing she shouldn't give a damn about his reaction but unable to help it. She'd wanted something more exclusive, sure, but given the timing… 'It was all I could get at short notice. We were lucky as it was to score a cancellation. And Monica's happy with the venue.' She stole a breath, paused for thought and wondered why it mattered. Damn the man! Why should she have to justify the choice of venue? 'Monica's more than happy, actually, because when all's said and done she just wants to marry Jake as soon as possible.'

She caught the flicker in his eyes, that tell-tale tic in his jaw even while he tried to put an appearance of civility over his hard, chiselled features, and she wondered again what the hell this was all about. Why his sudden interest in the arrangements? Why the sudden change of heart that meant he could even contemplate his sister's wedding?

Especially when it was crystal clear that he found the idea of his sister marrying Jake repugnant.

Sure, he'd been taken by surprise by his sister's news—but to go from being vehemently opposed to the match to suddenly being so interested in the details of the wedding seemed too good to be true. It *had* to be too good to be true.

She crossed her arms over her slim briefcase in front of her. 'What is this all about, Mr Caruana? And this time I'd appreciate a straight answer.'

He smiled, if you could call it that. 'I want to show you something—a place better befitting any marriage of my sister.'

'I just told you, we have a venue. Monica—'

'You have a golf club.'

'It's a reception centre.'

'It's old, overrated and it's not good enough, not for Monica. It's too public, it's too cheap.'

'Monica and Jake are working to a budget on this.'

'As head of Monica's family, I should be paying for my sister's wedding. People will expect it. You will make me look cheap.'

'I'm sorry.' She turned away, unable to listen any longer; she'd heard enough. Did Mr Impossible care about nothing but himself and the impression he made? 'It may surprise you to know that this wedding isn't actually about you.'

'Maybe not, but everyone will assume that I am paying. The press will have a field day, claiming that Daniel Caruana spends less on his sister's wedding than on his latest mistress.'

She closed her eyes, trying not to think too hard about what it would be like to be Daniel Caruana's mistress—and not because of the money he must throw at them. He would be an uncompromising lover, she imagined, hard, demanding and as ruthless in the bedroom as in the boardroom. What would it be like to be that close to him, to be the one to rake her nails across that broad, sculpted chest?

Not that she cared.

Liar.

If she didn't care, a menacing voice inside her questioned, then why had she even thought of it? Unless she was still remembering that whisper of a kiss and how it had made her tremble all the way to her toes...

'I wouldn't have thought,' she said, battling a mouth that suddenly felt too dry to extract the words she needed, 'that you were the type of man who worried about what anyone said, let alone the press.'

'There are some things,' he started, leaning towards her, his dark eyes like a promise and his voice like a glove that stroked velvet down her spine, 'that are so private they have no place in the press.'

Under an indigo sky and a sun so warm that her skin felt kissed by the very air, still she shivered with the force of his words. Or was it their content? Whatever it was, it was threatening to scramble her brain.

'Let me show you an alternative,' he suggested. 'A mere ten minute flight away,' he said, jerking her back to the present, reminding her of what they were doing here. 'No more.'

'Look, Mr Caruana.' She shook her head, trying to clear her thoughts, wishing she could rid herself of this infernal

instability that seemed to beleaguer her while he was anywhere near, 'I told you, we have a booking. I hardly see the
point.'

'Indulge me.' His voice performed that velvet glove stroke
down her spine again. She fought against a melting spine and
glanced at her watch, because she had to look somewhere and
if she looked into his eyes and saw that he'd meant his words
to have that reaction, she would be lost. She didn't want to
think about indulging Daniel Caruana in any way, shape or
form.

'The longer you argue,' he pressed, 'the longer it will be
before you get back to the airport for your return flight. You
do want to make that return flight, don't you?'

She snapped her head up. 'I don't have to come with
you.'

He appeared totally nonplussed by her outburst. 'I can
assure you, when you do come, your time won't be wasted.
On the way you can fill me in on all the details I didn't give
you a chance to tell me in our earlier meeting.'

She looked at her watch before realising she'd just done
that and taken no notice of the time, before looking back up
at the man she suspected of playing games with her without
bothering to fill her in on the rules. But she had come to
Cairns to try to reconcile him to the notion of Monica and
Jake's marrying; if he was even now contemplating that the
wedding might happen, then maybe he wasn't entirely a lost
cause. And maybe her day hadn't been a complete waste of
effort.

If she left now without getting his agreement to walk his
sister down the aisle, what would she tell Jake and Monica
when they called later tonight—that she had failed them because she was scared of Monica's brother?

She had no choice when it all came down to it. There were
still a couple of hours before she had to be back at the airport

for her scheduled flight. What did it matter if she didn't get an earlier one when Monica and Jake were relying on her to make this wedding happen? She couldn't let them down.

She kicked up her chin. 'And maybe I might even get my phone back?'

'But of course,' he said, handing it over with a smile that spoke of victory and made her wonder if whatever she was conceding was worth much more than the price of a mere mobile phone. 'You only had to ask.'

CHAPTER FIVE

Sophie wasted no time calling the airline to confirm her flight time, ensuring Daniel was within earshot when she repeated the time by which she had to check in so he could not pretend later that he hadn't known. There was no way she intended to miss her flight, especially when she wasn't at all convinced at the necessity for this side trip.

Daniel merely smiled and excused himself, walking a little distance away as he made his own brief call before they both climbed into the waiting helicopter.

The ground fell away below along with Sophie's stomach as the helicopter rose effortlessly above the palm trees and set out towards the nearby coast. Beneath them the land slipped behind, houses and buildings giving way to a border of palm-studded sand and a sea that lapped at its shores in various shades from pale blue to aqua to turquoise. Once again she was struck with the sheer force of colour; the sand was bleached to a startling white, the waters so bright and beautiful, while the densely tangled, forested mountains behind were a bold contrast of green.

It was breathtaking, almost as breathtaking as the man alongside her and his unexpected about-face and subsequent apology.

Never in a million years would she have expected an apology from someone like Daniel Caruana. The man had appeared a complete Neanderthal just this morning. Surely evolution was meant to take longer?

Maybe, like he said, he'd been taken unawares with the news of his little sister's wedding? That at least made some kind of sense. She had to admit, she'd been taken aback too with the suddenness of the announcement. In some ways she'd been frightened she was losing the brother she'd only recently found. It was only when Monica had made it plain that she'd never be excluded from Jake's life again, and she realised that the other woman meant it, that she'd really come to embrace the news herself.

Had Daniel similarly been afraid of losing Monica?

Is that why he'd ultimately changed his mind—because he was genuinely worried he'd put his own relationship with his sister at risk by refusing her right to decide who to marry?

Who could tell how Daniel Caruana's mind worked? After all, this was the man who paid off his sister's prospective suitors. Did he really care anything about her happiness?

Besides, she hadn't missed his reaction when she'd mentioned Jake's name before boarding the helicopter. It was clear that what he felt for her brother bordered on hatred. So, while on the surface he seemed more amenable to this wedding, nothing had changed there.

And nothing explained why he had all but kissed her. Her lips tingled at the memory, at the remembered heat of his proximity.

It had been little more than a brush of lips, as brief as it was unexpected, and then he'd wheeled away and turned his back on her as if it had been the biggest mistake of his life. What had that been about, if not a blatant, testosterone-driven attempt to try to scuttle her thoughts and arguments and show her who was boss?

And it had so very nearly worked.

She felt a tap on her arm and jumped, as if she'd summoned his attention with her thoughts, and she was thankful beyond measure that he couldn't read them.

He pointed now, and yelled something at her she couldn't quite catch over her headphones, but she followed where he was pointing and understood.

Just a smudge of bluish green appeared on the horizon, with a zig-zag line jutting into the sky. But she recognised the shape immediately. So that was Kallista. She remembered seeing pictures of it years ago in an article about the private playgrounds of Australia's rich and famous. She'd never thought for a moment that one day she'd be setting foot on it herself.

The island sat like a jewel just off the coast, plump green hillsides and jagged peaks sliding to blindingly white sand beaches thickly fringed with palms, and ringed with the coral reef that made the sea around the island appear a thousand different shades of blue.

As they circled the mountains, even more treasure was revealed. A lagoon on one side, the water so clear she could see fish darting to and fro in the shallows.

Sophie's heart sank.

It was tropical perfection.

It made the Tropical Palms golf course look like a shabby try-hard.

What bride wouldn't prefer to get married in such a picture-postcard setting?

But they had a booking and Monica was happy, she reminded herself. And it would be perfect on the day. It was Sophie's job to ensure it would be so.

'So what do you think?' Daniel asked, after landing, as they strolled along the short jetty towards a waiting golf buggy.

His eyes were hidden behind his sunglasses, his white-teeth smile wide, the smile of a man who assumed he'd already won the battle, if not the war.

She looked anywhere but at him as they reached the buggy. 'It's nice,' she said with a nod, probably making the under-statement of the year, but she wasn't about to gush, not when he would take any encouragement she offered as support for his plans to shift the venue from Brisbane to the island.

'Nice?' he repeated, rolling the word around his mouth like it had left a bad taste. 'You don't think you could be just a little more enthusiastic?'

She looked around. 'Well, it's got a lovely beach and loads of palm trees.'

'Monica loves this island,' he insisted. 'She always said that one day she wanted to get married here.'

Sophie didn't doubt it; no wonder Monica had specified palm trees and sunsets on her must-have list. She imagined the sunsets here must be something to behold. But what she did doubt was Daniel's conviction about wanting there to be a wedding at all, let alone playing host to it. For someone who had seemed so vehemently opposed to the idea just a few short hours ago, now it seemed he wanted control of the entire event.

And why? Because he was so happy he wanted his sister's wedding to be perfect? She seriously doubted it. His turn-around had been too quick, too contrived.

Too convenient.

Something was going on, if only she could work out what it was.

But one thing was clear—there was no way she'd agree to Kallista being the venue for the wedding. Jake had made it clear he'd prefer the wedding to be on neutral ground. She'd thought it a strange thing to specify at first, but having met

Daniel and witnessed his animosity towards her brother she could see where Jake was coming from. Daniel was the sort of man you had to stand up to, or get railroaded in the process.

She turned back to him, determined not to be railroaded herself. 'Okay, you're right, it is a beautiful island—perfect, I guess, if you want to plan on getting married barefoot on the sand. But in terms of infrastructure for a wedding?' She shrugged. 'For a start you'd have to have catering and accommodation facilities. Unless you'd be happy to boat everything in and lug everyone back and forth to the mainland on either a launch or—' she nodded towards the helicopter '—that thing.'

She could swear she could see the glint in his eyes even through the dark glasses. 'That won't be necessary.' He banged his hand on the top of the buggy. 'Climb in. I will let you judge if Kallista has the necessary *infrastructure*.'

Sophie did as he asked, climbing into the front seat beside him without bothering to tell him about the article she'd read all those years ago citing a house set high above the sea nestled amongst the vines and palms. Just one house. Sprawling around the hillside, perhaps, but barely enough to cater for an entire wedding party and guests.

Neither did she bother to repeat that there was no point to this entire trip anyway. Tomorrow morning she would pay the deposit that would secure the Tropical Palms golf club, as Monica and Jake had agreed, and Daniel Caruana could go to hell. What did he know about what was needed to organise a wedding? The Tropical Palms might be in need of refurbishment, but if he thought his sister was going to be happy to put up with marquees and sand flies on her special day he could think again.

The buggy took off along the track carved through the sands, heading for the shade of the palms. Somewhere along the line he'd undone the cuffs of his shirt and turned them up, exposing his forearms, his bronzed olive skin making his white shirt look more dramatic as the soft material billowed softly in the breeze. Suddenly she was transported back to her childhood and B-movie matinees featuring swashbuckling pirates with tight breeches, white shirts and gold rings in one ear.

He could almost be a pirate, she thought, with his midnight-black hair, his strong features and his arrogant, 'it's my way or the plank way' attitude.

The buggy's tiny tyres bumped over a fallen palm frond, the vehicle swaying as he immediately rounded a bend, a bubble of laughter erupted unbidden from her throat.

Almost a pirate—but for the fact she'd never thought of a pirate driving a golf buggy before.

'Is something funny?'

She pressed her lips together, looked at the track in front of them and avoided his gaze, even when she sensed it burning holes in her. 'It's just I saw your car—the black one you were leaning on where we met the helicopter.'

'And?'

'And it looked exactly like what I'd imagined you'd drive.'

'Oh, and what's that?'

The tiny vehicle rattled along the track. 'You know, something sleek and black and…' *Dangerous.* She stopped herself just in time 'And fast.'

'And that's funny?'

'Well, no, not really, it's just that—' She faltered, suddenly wondering why she'd ever been crazy enough to open her mouth. Next she'd be admitting she could imagine him as a pirate with a cutlass in one hand, a rope from the rigging in the other and a dagger shoved in his belt. And wouldn't that do her cause a power of good? She looked up at him, thankful for the shade from the canopy above them so he wouldn't be able to see the colour flooding her cheeks as she dreaded how he might react to the words she was game to put voice to. 'It's just that I guess I never imagined a man like you driving a golf buggy.'

He didn't get angry like she'd expected. Instead his lips curved upwards before he turned to her. 'I bet there are a lot of things you never imagined a man like me doing.'

He held her eyes for a fraction too long, an unnecessary fraction, before he turned his attention back to the weaving track.

She was so glad in that moment that he couldn't possibly read her thoughts, because then he might know that already she'd imagined him doing plenty.

He wondered what she'd been going to say when she faltered, wondered what she was thinking now; if he didn't know better, he'd think she was blushing. 'As it happens,' he admitted, 'I do have a thing for sleek, black and—' he threw her a glance '—fast cars. But here on the island this is how we get around. I'm sorry if it's not sleek and black and fast enough for you.'

His smile widened. She was blushing—even under the dappled light her face was flooded with colour—but this time she wasn't angry, he was sure of it, by the way her eyes wanted to avoid him rather than impale him. In fact, if he didn't know better, he'd even have thought Miss 'Prim'n'Proper' Turner had caught herself out. What had she been thinking? The way she was sitting up now, so stiff backed and straitlaced, she could have been a Victorian spinster school teacher on her way to meet her new school in a village full of head hunters.

But she wasn't as strait-laced and spinsterish as she liked to make out, he knew that first hand. She'd been no unbendable block of concrete in his hands. Instead, she'd felt all woman, a combination of tantalising dips and sweet curves, her feminine scent beguiling, her lips a silken caress.

He almost growled at the memory. And she was here now, on his island, *in his territory*. How would Fletcher react to that news? An eye for an eye, a sister for a sister.

Which reminded him...

'How is it your name is Turner?'

'Excuse me?' She swung her head round but not before he'd noticed how the breeze shook tendrils of her hair loose to curl around her face and sculpt the soft fabric of her dress so it clung to her breasts and playfully teased around her knees. Then she noticed the direction of his eyes and tucked the wayward material under her legs. He didn't mind that either, because now it only highlighted the elegant tapering of thigh to knees.

Long, shapely legs. Nice breasts. He could only imagine what other treats the surprising Miss Turner had in store. A pity, really...

'You're name's Turner,' he said, pulling his thoughts back into line. 'Not Fletcher. But you weren't married, you said, or at least you're not now. Fletcher never mentioned having a sister.'

She hesitated, and he sensed the cogs in her brain working out his angle. She didn't trust him, that much was obvious, although she was beginning to lose a little of that abrasive defensiveness. All that talk about what kind of car he drove— she'd been thinking about him, and he'd lay odds she hadn't been thinking about automobiles. Finally, when he'd almost given up on a response, he picked up her shrug in his peripheral vision.

'It's no big secret,' she began on a sigh, almost as if resigned to the fact he'd find out eventually anyway. 'Our parents separated when I was barely a year old, splitting everything in two, including the kids. Dad kept Jake, Mum took me. She changed my name to hers, I guess so she didn't have a constant reminder of her ex. I didn't know about any of it for years.'

The gears in Daniel's mind crunched. So she was Fletcher's sister, as she'd claimed. Jo's digging would confirm it, but he had no doubt she was telling the truth. Which meant that she probably was in on whatever her brother had planned to make this so-called marriage look as legitimate as possible in order to extract the best settlement. 'So, how did you two find each other again?'

The buggy sped along the narrow track. Glimpses of brilliant sunshine and a sapphire sea appeared only to be swallowed up again by the foliage.

'Mum died two years ago. Some lawyer told me then that I had a brother. I'd had no idea. I was too young to remember anything. We met for the first time at her funeral. And that's when I learned that our father had died ten years before. My mother never…'

Her voice broke. He glanced over, but she wasn't looking at him, her eyes appeared fixed on some point ahead of them as she took a deep breath, her breasts rising under the slip of silk.

'Anyway, that's the whole gruesome story.'

She sounded so lost and alone in that instant that it was his turn to take a deep breath. Next thing he knew, he'd be feeling sorry for her—Fletcher's sister, of all people! Besides, he remembered seeing Jake's old man once, sitting on the veranda of their timber house. The place had been practically falling down around him while he'd sucked his beer dry, the empties scattered around him like toppled ninepins. It was no surprise to hear that he'd gone.

Maybe it was better she'd never met him. She might have ended up more like her brother. A brother she defended like a tiger would defend her cubs. Would she be so quick to defend him if she knew more of his past? He doubted it.

'So, you haven't actually known Fletcher that long?'

Her jawline hardened, her mouth tightening. 'I've known him long enough.'

'Maybe you don't know him as well as you think.'

'Look, Mr Caruana, I think we've established how you feel about my brother.'

'Daniel.'

'What?'

'Didn't we agree you'd call me Daniel? And that I would call you by your first name?'

'I—'

'After all, Sophie,' he argued softly, slowing the vehicle for a bend, 'We *are* almost related.'

She sat upright in her seat, even stiffer and more tight-lipped than before, and he got the distinct impression she considered the idea of him being her brother-in-law with even less appeal than he contemplated her becoming his sister-in-law, though why that notion should grate he wasn't entirely sure.

They rounded the last curve and he heard her small gasp of surprise beside him as the first timber and palm bungalow came into view with the hint of more hidden in the dense palm forest beyond. 'What's this?'

He jerked on the handbrake and jumped out, offering her his hand. 'You said you wanted *infrastructure*,' he mocked. 'And I always give a lady what she wants.'

She'd just bet he did. Although her cynicism would have been far more effective if his words had not just sent a burst of heat all the way down her spine.

'Don't worry about your things,' he said as she reached for her briefcase. 'The only people on the island are my employees. They know if they do anything wrong, they'll be FBO'd.'

'"FBO'd"?' she asked, keeping the rising panic from her voice as reluctantly she put her hand in his, feeling his warm fingers wrap around her hand, feeling his strength, his heat and his sheer masculine power as he helped her out of the buggy. It didn't help that he was smiling. It didn't help that she could feel that smile all the way down to her toes.

Surely it shouldn't feel so good to touch someone who was so arrogant and unlikeable, someone who made clear his feelings that her brother was in no way good enough to marry his sister? Then he let her hand go to indicate she precede him up the steps to the timber deck, and she had to clamp down on a bizarre sense of disappointment. 'What does FBO mean, exactly?' she asked with false brightness, wishing she had either her briefcase or portfolio to cling onto, anything to make her hands feel less awkward and empty as she climbed the short flight of steps up to the deck, skirted a table and two chairs and stood by the railing, looking out at the view.

He came alongside her where the bungalow looked out through the thinning spread of trees towards the sandy beach and the promise of oceanic perfection.

'It means they'll be on the first boat off.'

'You mean like on those reality shows where someone gets voted off the island?'

'There's no voting involved,' he said unapologetically, crossing the deck to slide big glass doors that opened to billowing curtains, standing back to let her pass. 'You mess up, you pay the price.'

She almost laughed. Almost. Until she caught his deadpan expression and realised he was completely and utterly serious. 'Sounds like a mantra to live by,' she murmured.

'It works for me,' he said simply, swiping off his sunglasses. As she moved past him she wondered if he was only talking about his employees.

This was Daniel's island and he was in charge. King of his island castle. Thank heavens Monica had agreed to hold the wedding in Brisbane. She couldn't imagine trying to organise a wedding here with Daniel watching, waiting for every mistake. Not that there was any chance of that happening, no matter what he thought of his 'infrastructure'.

Sophie entered the bure, removed her sunglasses and felt her heart sink as her eyes adjusted. The sight of the bungalows hidden in the rainforest had been a surprise in itself; the article she'd read had mentioned nothing of scattered bungalows. But, while the decking had been thoughtfully designed, the simple exterior had given no indication of the luxury contained within. The timber-framed glass doors opened straight into a spacious sitting-room decorated not in the usual and unimaginative palm-tree prints but in tasteful russet, cream and coffee shades. The prints on fabrics and walls were minimal, the furnishings inviting, and Sophie applauded every decorating choice.

In a wall opposite the entry, bi-fold doors beckoned, hinging back to reveal a bedroom even larger than the living area with a pillow-laden bed so wide and inviting that the child in her was tempted to dive straight onto it. Sophie would have too, until her adult brain reminded her that Daniel was just behind her. Any sign of enthusiasm now was only going to make it more difficult for herself later on when she had to argue that this venue wouldn't work.

She still believed it, even with the glimpse of more bures tucked between the trees. A few cabins, after all, did not make a resort. The catering facilities would have to be first rate too, though a niggle in the back of her brain told her that bures of this standard would require more than a simple barbeque on the beach every night. But whatever they were like, she told herself, the inspection was pointless. They had a venue. End of story.

'Very nice,' she conceded with a terse nod, schooling her face to bland, knowing Daniel was waiting for her reaction. Another door led to the adjoining bathroom with spa bath and rainforest shower head which she eyed with as much detachment and as little envy as she could manage.

But there was no denying the sudden stab of guilt. It was gorgeous, seriously gorgeous, and she couldn't have blamed Monica in the least if she'd wanted to get married here on the island. She didn't know what else was in store for this inspection, but a bit of dressing up could turn a bure like this into every girl's fantasy honeymoon suite.

Her teeth scraped her bottom lip as she recalled the rooms at the Tropical Palms. Outdated. Bordering on shabby. Seriously in need of refurbishment. Whereas here…

Jake had wanted the wedding to take place in Brisbane and Monica had agreed to the Tropical Palms because she'd thought Daniel would never agree to her marriage, that he would never tolerate it, let alone offer to pay for it. And also, she had to admit, because it was the only place going at short notice that could offer a taste of the tropical paradise that Kallista was.

What if Daniel was right and Monica had always wanted to be married here? Right now she only had Daniel's word on that, but looking around it didn't take too much stretch of the imagination to believe it.

Had Monica suppressed her heart's desire to be married here on Kallista because she had thought it would present the path of least resistance and accommodate both her brother's and her fiancé's wishes?

Which left her—as a wedding planner who promised a perfect day—where, exactly?

'So, what do you think?'

She wheeled around so quickly that her head spun. Was it just the sight of him reclining on the side of the bed behind her and not waiting in the doorway like she'd expected? Her mouth went dry. His eyes were level with her breasts. She knew that because he was looking right at them. And once again she cursed the absence of anything she could hold up against her chest as a shield to hide her suddenly achingly hard nipples.

'About what?'

He glanced up at her eyes, looking for all the world like a predator at ease, propped up on one elbow against the pillow-decked headrest, all long-limbed elegance sprawled ever so casually and yet with a barely suppressed energy just waiting to be unleashed.

'About whatever you've been thinking about this last five minutes you've been staring into space.'

She swallowed, attempted a smile and was sure it came off as too contrived, but she was still too thrown by the picture of him lounging ever so casually against the wide bed to know how to compensate. If he looked that good dressed, lying on a big, wide bed, how much better would he look undressed?

Oh, no!

She knew in that moment that there was no way—*no way*—she wanted this wedding to take place here on Kallista. Her thoughts would be forever distracted by pictures of Daniel sprawled back against the bedding, or with the fine cotton of his shirt rippling against his bronzed olive skin as the warm wind tugged at the fabric, or with him just being there.

So she made a show of checking her watch and flashing her brightest, most meaningless smile. 'I think we better get on with the inspection if I'm going to make my flight.'

It was as bad as she expected. There were twenty such bures, all just as superbly appointed. They were tucked between the palms around the lagoon with enough distance between them to make you think you were the only inhabitants on the island, plus there was a central long house that served as lounge-bar and restaurant.

It was worse than bad, she decided, sipping on a mango cocktail and overlooking a crystal clear pool set amidst the palms.

It was an absolute disaster.

It was perfect.

Or it could be, if not for the man sitting opposite her right now.

Daniel Caruana leaned smugly back in his chair like he thought he had the whole world and not just his sister's wedding stitched up.

Sophie was more and more fearful that he did—at least, when it came to the wedding. After all, this was a man used to fighting and winning corporate battles every day, used to manoeuvring against major players in the boardroom and beating them at their own game. How was she supposed to hold her own against the likes of him?

'I guess we should be heading to the helicopter soon,' she suggested, 'if I'm going to make my flight.'

'I guess we should,' he said, leaning back and crossing his arms behind his head as if he had no intention of going anywhere. 'Except…' He smiled. 'You haven't told me what you think of my *infrastructure* yet.'

She sipped her drink, gazing as inconspicuously as possible over the rim of her glass at the broad expanse of chest under the snug-fitting shirt. There was nothing at all wrong with his infrastructure from where she was sitting; the man was a perfect specimen, fit, strong and sexy as sin, and that was putting it mildly. Not that she was about to admit it. 'I didn't expect to find the island so developed. I was under the impression there was just the one dwelling.'

He dropped his hands to his front, lacing his fingers over an impossibly flat stomach. Did the man not have an ounce of fat anywhere? 'It seemed selfish to keep all this to myself.'

'But there's nobody here but us and a handful of staff, and you don't operate as a resort. What's it all for?'

He shrugged. 'Caruana Corporation has many employees who require the usual training and professional development. Sometimes they come for team-building exercises, sometimes as incentives. One group of managers has just left this morning. Another team will arrive next week. A skeleton staff keeps the place ticking over in between.'

'But it looks like a five-star complex. You must have spent a fortune on this place.'

He leaned forwards, his elbow on the table, his fingers out wide to support his point. 'And why pay a fortune for them to go somewhere else when I have my own island just off the coast? But what I have spent is not your concern. What I am more interested in is whether you now agree that this is the perfect place to host Monica's wedding.'

It *was* a perfect venue. There was enough accommodation for plenty of the nearest and dearest with the best accommodation that Far North Queensland had to offer just a short helicopter flight or launch ride away. Absolutely perfect, except for one not quite so small fly in the ointment.

Daniel Caruana.

'Mr Caruana?' she began.

'Why do you have so much trouble calling me Daniel?'

She sucked in air. Did he mean apart from the fact it seemed so informal? Too personal? 'Okay—Daniel. You're right, it is a fabulous venue. And I'm sure it would be perfect in the right circumstances. But maybe not this time. I've already told you, we have a venue, and one which Monica and Jake have both agreed on.'

'So cancel it.'

'Excuse me?'

'Cancel the venue and save the money. You said Monica and Fletcher were working to a budget—this venue won't cost them a cent.'

She breathed deep. She had to in order to give herself time to think. Everything he said made perfect sense. The venue was divine, the accommodation superb and she had no doubt the food would be exquisite. All that, and Jake and Monica could save themselves a bundle into the deal. She must be mad to be so desperate to find a reason to say no. But Daniel was so adamant—disturbingly so—and there was no way she was being railroaded into saying yes, certainly not before she'd had a chance to speak to her clients.

Monica might well be in love with the idea of getting married on the island, but Sophie only had Daniel's word for that. Meanwhile her own brother, she knew, had other ideas about what constituted a perfect venue. Daniel Caruana's private island was hardly likely to fit the bill on that score.

'Look,' she ventured, glad she'd never shared the fact that the deposit on the Tropical Palms hadn't yet been paid. 'It's very short notice and there may be penalties for cancellation that reduce any potential savings. But I'll certainly speak to both Monica and Jake regarding your generous offer.' She glanced at her watch, shocked to see how time had slipped away, and stood, collecting up her things. 'I have to go. I have an early morning meeting tomorrow and I'm not prepared to miss that flight.' And then, because she knew she had to offer him something, 'How about I call you tomorrow? Let you know what Monica and Jake are thinking?'

A hand on her arm stopped her flight and she jumped. 'And how about we discuss it now?'

She looked up at him, his brow was brooding over dark narrowed eyes and a jaw set like concrete. She tested his grip with just one tiny tug on her arm and found no give, no weakness. 'I can't afford to miss my flight.'

'Why are you so opposed to holding the wedding here?'

She swallowed. 'Can you blame me for being a little reluctant to agree to your every whim? May I remind you that you were the one who said there would *be* no wedding?'

He made a sound like a growl. 'We've been through that. Getting married here is what Moni really wants.'

'And we have a booking Monica agreed to. Somewhere else.'

'This is my sister we're talking about.'

'And Monica is my client. I've acted in accordance with her wishes. Thank you for your advice and your tour, Mr Caruana; I will pass on your thoughts to my client, but I'm afraid I must leave. I have a plane to catch.' She looked pointedly down at the hand that still maintained an iron grip on her arm. 'If you wouldn't mind?'

He said nothing, but she sensed his anger in his heated breath, in the flare of his nostrils as his chest expanded with every intake of air and in the red-hot brand of his fingers pressing into her arm.

It was only her arm he was holding, she had to remind herself, so why did her skin prickle from her scalp to her toes? And why did heat ribbon and curl in dark and secret places until she was sure she would ignite?

Then something sparked in his eyes and he let her go so suddenly she almost lost her balance. 'As you wish. I will take you to the helicopter.'

Breath whooshed into her lungs as she regained her balance. 'Thank you.' But she doubted he heard her. He was already striding away when her phone rang.

She pulled her mobile from her bag and checked the number, breathing a sigh of relief that it was Meg at the office calling and not a new client looking for the perfect day—the only perfect daze she was qualified to talk about right now was the one she was currently in.

'Meg, what's up? I'm on my way to the airport right now.'

Her assistant took her own sweet time answering—long enough for Daniel to have come looking for her, no doubt wondering why someone so desperate to leave was now dragging her feet. She turned away from his storm-cloud presence. 'Meg? What's wrong?'

'That all depends,' came the tentative response. 'Do you want the good news or the bad news?'

CHAPTER SIX

SOPHIE swallowed. Things went pear-shaped in the wedding planner business all the time—wedding cakes missing a layer, string quartets going their own separate ways and citing irreconcilable differences, limousines breaking down. There wasn't much they hadn't seen and there wasn't much they couldn't deal with. So why Meg sounded so shell shocked…

'So, what's the good news?'

'You don't have an eight a.m. meeting tomorrow morning at the Gold Coast any more.'

'What? Okay, what time is it scheduled for then?'

She could almost hear Meg's anguish in the silent prelude to her reply. 'Well, that's kind of the bad news. You don't need another time. They've cancelled the booking.'

'*Cancelled*? But they can't do that!'

'I'm sorry, Sophie, I really am. But a girl—Annaliese, I think she said her name was—just called and said they had someone who could book out the entire function centre, not just the gazebo and reception room, and they paid up front in full so they had no choice but to take it.'

'But they can't do that,' she repeated. *Surely they couldn't do that?* 'I'll call them. Annaliese is only new there. She probably got her dates mixed up.'

'Good luck,' came Meg's voice down the line. 'Only she sounded so certain. I hope you're right.'

'Problem?' Daniel's voice intruding into her thoughts was the last thing she needed right now. Daniel's presence was the last thing she needed, point blank.

'Excuse me a moment,' she said, drawing away, needing distance. 'I have to make an urgent call.'

He made an exaggerated play of checking the gold watch at his wrist, a small frown creasing his brow. 'You did say you had a plane to catch.'

'I'm sorry,' she hissed, wheeling away. 'Please, this won't take long.'

Her mind was racing, her heart thumping loud in her chest as she retrieved the number. Her teeth gnawed at her bottom lip as she waited in turn for the connection, then the pick-up, and then the seemingly interminable wait for the transfer to the functions manager. She registered the metallic taste of blood, realised her lip was stinging, and willed herself to take a deep breath to relax. At this rate she could chew her way right down to her jaw.

The Tropical Palms had to be available. Someone had merely made a mistake. Otherwise…

Forget otherwise.

'Philipe!' she cried with relief when finally the connection was made, hope reborn. 'I just heard the craziest thing. I thought I should double check.'

A bare minute later she severed the connection, Philipe's rapid-fire excuses buzzing in her head.

'Sincere apologies.' 'If only you'd already paid the deposit.' 'Our hands are tied'…

Numbly she turned. Sure, she'd understood that her booking wouldn't be solid until the deposit was paid, but they'd given no hint of any other interest in the date, and it had been Philipe who'd told her not to worry—that paying when she came for the meeting would be early enough. They could at least have called and warned her someone wanted to book out the entire complex. They could at least have let her know.

'Trouble in paradise?'

She gritted her teeth, wishing she was back in the office right now. Somewhere she could throw things. Instead she had to put up with a smiling inquisitor while trying to ignore the prick of tears. What the hell was she supposed to tell Monica and Jake? 'Nothing I can't handle,' she sniffed as she headed past him towards where he'd left the buggy.

'No?' he said, already catching up and way, way too close for comfort. 'I couldn't help but overhear. I got the impression it was more serious than that.'

'It'll be fine.' It had to be fine. It *would* be fine, just as soon as she could get away from Daniel Caruana and think.

'It was about Monica's wedding, wasn't it? I take it that was the venue you just called?'

She shook her head, breathing deep as a day filled with frustration after frustration forced a renegade tear from her eye. Damn it, but she would not cry. Not here, not in front of him. 'It's between me and my clients. It's got nothing to do with you.'

'It has if it concerns my sister!' She felt a hand on her shoulder, felt herself hauled around to face him. 'What's going on?' He paused, lifted the hand from her shoulder and touched the pad of his thumb to her cheek even as she turned her face away. But nothing could stop the jolt of electricity that sparked through her at his touch. 'You're crying. Was it such bad news?'

She jerked her head away, swiping at the dampness on her cheek. 'I am not crying.' But her voice was shaky, her breath was choppy, and she knew that he would have had to be blind, deaf and dumb not to notice. Besides, it wasn't as if she could keep the news some kind of secret. She sucked in a deep breath. 'The Tropical Palms apparently got a better offer. We've lost the venue.'

He took less a second to assimilate the information before nodding decisively. 'Then the matter is settled. You will arrange the wedding here.'

She blinked away her tears. 'Now, just hold on. It's not actually up to you.'

'And you have a better idea? Other options?'

'I haven't explored the other options yet.'

'I've just saved you the trouble.'

'We could still get a cancellation.' But she knew she was clutching at straws.

'Is that what you're planning on telling Monica? That you're waiting for a cancellation when she could be married here, on Kallista?'

She looked up at him, just for a second wondering—was it just coincidence that on the very day she met with Daniel Caruana her plans for his sister's wedding had gone pear-shaped? He'd been determined the wedding should take place here. Was it possible that he was somehow behind the sudden booking? 'I told you where the wedding was to be held before we took off.'

'And?'

'And isn't it a coincidence that suddenly I find someone's come along and booked out the entire function centre at the exact same time you're arguing for the wedding to be held here?'

He leaned an arm up on the roof of the buggy, so close to her shoulder that she wanted to shrink away. 'You think I did it?' His tone made her sound completely paranoid. Maybe she was. It was too easy to believe Daniel would go to whatever lengths it took to get his way. Then again, maybe she wasn't so paranoid. How could she trust him after the massive about-face he'd made today? It was clear that if this wedding was to go ahead he expected it to be on his terms.

She cocked her chin. 'Didn't you?'

'And when exactly was I supposed to have made this booking when I have been with you the entire time?'

It was the question she'd been battling with herself. 'I don't know. But you did make a phone call, just before we left the mainland.'

Something skated across his eyes. 'And there would be no other possible reason for me to make a phone call, not even to inform the island to have a buggy waiting for us by the helipad?'

She wanted the ground to open up and swallow her. She sounded worse than paranoid; now she was practically blaming him for losing the booking. 'I'm sorry. But what else was I supposed to think? You've been determined to have this wedding here ever since you accepted that there was nothing you could do to prevent it.'

'I just want what's best for Monica. I suspect you do too. Which is why maybe we should be working on this together.'

'What do you mean?'

'I think when Monica calls from Honolulu we should both be there to talk to her—find out what she really wants to do. And maybe put her mind at rest that I'm serious about having the wedding on Kallista.'

She shook her head. 'I don't see how. It could be a while before she calls, given even after they land they'll have to clear customs before their hotel transfer. I'll probably be back in Brisbane by then.'

'Then don't leave. Stay here, on Kallista.'

Sophie blinked, his seemingly simple words performing cartwheels over and over in her head, her thoughts in turmoil.

How could she stay when she wanted nothing more than to be out of this man's company as soon as possible? Already once today that escape had been denied her, pulled from beneath her feet as effectively as the proverbial rug.

But she wanted Monica and Jake happy and, now her morning meeting with the Tropical Palms had been cancelled, it wasn't as if she had to be back in time for the commute to the Gold Coast first thing tomorrow.

It was the last thing she wanted, but maybe she should delay her departure a little longer. There was a lot to be said for Monica knowing her brother was more supportive of the marriage than she'd anticipated, and perhaps Jake might benefit from hearing it too. Perhaps this was actually what everyone needed, a chance to talk things through and get over whatever it was in the past that was potentially such a barrier. After all, if they were going to be family, they'd all have to learn to communicate with each other some time.

And after the call maybe there might be a red-eye that would still get her back to Brisbane tonight.

Please God she could get back home tonight. It could be hours that she was forced to hang around waiting for Monica's call. And the longer she was in Daniel Caruana's company the more his presence messed with her head, muddled her brain and her thought processes along with it, even while setting her other senses alight. It wasn't a state she was used to. It wasn't a state she particularly enjoyed.

She was used to being in control, cool, detached and unaffected. Her mother had taught her that a woman didn't need a man to validate her, in fact that sometimes she would be better off without one. While she knew her mother's view had stemmed from a failed marriage, and a couple of aborted relationships since, her own experiences with men had only lent weight to her mother's advice.

Which had proved a positive boon to her job. She could stand back unemotionally and deliver the best, most romantic wedding in the world without getting all misty-eyed herself. She was the practical one, the unemotional one. The rational one.

Until now.

Until Daniel Caruana.

Oh no; it would be better—*safer*—to be gone.

Daniel watched the indecision swirl in her violet eyes. She was gnawing her bottom lip again, a gesture that took years off her. She looked young and vulnerable. Her hair was loosened by the breeze so that tendrils had escaped, wisping around her face, and he had the insane desire to kiss her again, if only to soothe her besieged lip.

He liked the way she tasted. He liked the way she battled with her conscience as she gnawed on that lip, and he couldn't help but wonder how it would feel if she turned those nibbling teeth on him.

He almost growled. There was no way she was leaving the island before he found out.

'What are you so afraid of?' he asked, moving closer, dropping his other arm to the vehicle behind. 'Why is it so hard to make a decision?'

She looked up at him, surprise at his sudden move turning her eyes wide, shock at finding herself trapped neatly against the vehicle when she tried shuffling backwards filling them with alarm. 'Oh, nothing. I'd have to call Meg at the office, get her to take care of a few things. And change my flight booking, of course, although I don't know what time I'll be able to get away.'

She was babbling, flustered again, and delightfully so. 'Is that all you're worried about?'

Her eyes darted from one side to the other, checking the positioning of his arms as if assessing her chances of escape.

Didn't she realise? *It was much too late for escape.*

'Or perhaps you're you worried I might kiss you?' He wanted her to be. If she hadn't been worried before, he wanted her thinking about his lips on hers right now. 'Is that what you're afraid of? Is that why you seem so desperate to rush off now, because you're afraid of a repeat performance?'

'What? No, why would I be worried about that? It never crossed my mind.'

'Never?' he murmured as he moved inexorably closer, the circle around her drawing tighter. 'You wound me, Miss Turner. You never once entertained the prospect of finishing what we started?'

'I never…' She shook her head but there was no point trying to deny it. Her eyes were on his lips; her chest was rising fast and her lips were slightly parted, waiting. *Anticipating.* 'You wouldn't—'

She didn't get a chance to finish. His mouth met hers, his lips relieving her of the word she'd been about to utter, her lips soft and warm and wondering. He sensed her doubts in her hesitation. But beyond that he also sensed her desire and her need.

It amazed him to think that any sister of Fletcher could taste as good. He expected there to be some trace of corruption, some hint of decay, and yet instead the taste of fruit was on her lips, plump and sweet as they moved under his, warm as their breath mingled. And wrapped seductively around it all he sensed the evocative scent of woman.

He made no attempt to hold her; they touched nowhere but at their mouths, and yet the connection was electric. He could feel the glow from her as if he'd flicked a switch that set her body humming with need, matching the music of his own. And yet it wasn't a kiss of passion, of unrequited lust. Instead it was tender and sweet and utterly, utterly necessary.

'Wh…why did you do that?' she whispered, her lashes lowered as if too scared to look at him when finally, reluctantly, he raised his head.

'It seemed a good idea to get it out of the way.'

'Oh.' It satisfied him no end that she sounded confused and halfway disappointed.

'Because now I know that first time wasn't a mistake.'

She gasped as her lashes flickered open, her pupils tiny in the bright sun; her irises seemed appropriately named given their suddenly dark, velvet colour. He laughed, because he knew that if he didn't he wouldn't be able to stop from pulling her back into his kiss and finishing what he'd begun. This wasn't the time, and definitely not the place. The sun beat down hot and heavy on his back, reinforcing his need for a cold beer and a cold shower—not necessarily in that order. 'Look, it's been a long day. Monica's probably not going to call for an hour or two. How about a swim to cool off while we wait? I know I could do with one.'

Her brow creased into a slight frown. 'Did I say I was staying?'

'Aren't you?'

She looked away then in the direction of the helipad, even though there was nothing to see from here but the thick tropical plantings of palms and bamboo bordering the parking area, before slowly she turned back. 'I guess I can stay, just for the call. But I haven't brought anything with me. I wasn't expecting to swim.'

'Not a problem,' he said, tossing the buggy key up in his hand. 'I'm sure we can find you something half decent.'

The house was halfway around the island and perched up high, all timber and glass, with decking and sails nestled amongst the forest and wrapped around the hillside. But despite the stunning beauty of the house it was the view to which the eye was drawn—on one side to the ocean, studded with island jewels, and on the other to the spectacular line of mainland coast that ran as far as the eye could see. Beyond the shoreline rose the steep mountains, the spectacular gateway to the hinterland.

'It's beautiful,' Sophie said as he helped her from the car. 'I don't know how you could ever bear to leave.'

He smiled that lazy crocodile smile once more, the smile aimed right at her, and that scored a direct hit. 'I'm glad you think so.' Breathless, not seeing or understanding the message she was sure lay behind the words, she moved away, pretending to be more interested in the view. It was magnificent, it was true, but right now she had more pressing things on her mind.

Like why she'd let him kiss her. She was planning his sister's wedding, after all. She was supposed to be a professional. She was supposed to be detached.

Letting him kiss her had hardly been detached.

But supposition was one thing. Knowing what she should do when he was looking at her that way, when her skin was tingling, her heart trembling and her thoughts as scattered as the winds was another thing entirely. How was she expected to think when all she knew was that she hungered for his kiss, that every cell in her body had been primed for his touch?

Was it only this morning they had met? It hardly seemed possible to reconcile the man who'd kissed her so tenderly with the man she'd encountered in his office—the man who'd turned arrogance into an art form and bundled her out without a decent hearing. Although he'd almost kissed her then too, practically reducing her to a puddle on the floor before she'd managed to find the will to push him away.

But had she pushed him away when he'd come back a second time? Oh no. Her body had been strung tight as a wire, not from dread or revulsion, but from the anticipation thrumming in her veins as she'd watched his mouth descend.

And the only thought in her mind was that there was no way she was going to stop him.

Far below them the azure sea lapped half-heartedly at a tiny cove of diamond-tipped water and a beach of brilliant white sand protected at either end by a rocky point jutting into the sea. Totally private and utterly inviting. It would be a long climb down the wooden steps she could see, but already she could feel the cool water sliding over her heated body.

Except would it really cool her down? Her teeth gnawed on her bottom lip as her mind churned over the implications. Was it really wise to strip down to a borrowed swimsuit and share the water with a man who was distracting enough with his clothes on, let alone wearing nothing more than bathers? She squeezed her eyes shut, desperate to extinguish the pictures that thought conjured up, of a body naked but for a band of black lycra. Oh no! A swim was a really bad idea.

'I think I might actually pass on the swimming after all,' she decided, searching for an excuse that didn't scream 'coward', and trying to pretend she wasn't more hot and bothered than ever. 'My heels would never last the climb down those steps. But you go right ahead.' When she looked up it was to find him not looking down at the cove, like she'd hoped, but still watching her. Heat flared in her cheeks, his unrelenting gaze unnerving, even while shrouded by sunglasses.

'I'd hate to risk your heels,' he said, half-smiling, as if he found her discomfiture amusing. 'So why not use the pool, like I intend to? I gather your heels are good for a few more metres.'

As if realising he'd won the point, he turned and led the way through the tangle of bougainvillea that spilled a riot of colour over the entrance to the courtyard, while Sophie followed meekly behind, feeling more of a fool than ever. Of course a house like this would have a pool tucked away somewhere, so what excuse was she going to dream up next without looking like she was afraid of getting into the water with him—that she was afraid of crocodiles?

Not that that would work, she decided, abandoning the idea as useless. Daniel was exactly the kind of man who would probably be flattered by such a comparison.

The timber entry door swung open before they reached it, and a middle-aged woman beamed at them under her apron. Sophie took to her warm and welcoming eyes on sight. 'Mr Caruana! You should have told me you were bringing back a guest,' she chided as they entered the spacious room, clearly with no qualms about castigating her boss over his lack of forward notice. 'I would have prepared something more special for dinner.'

'I'm sure whatever you have planned, Millie, will be superb as usual. And I have no doubt Miss Turner here will soon likewise be a fan of your cooking.' He turned to Sophie. 'Millie used to run a café in Cairns, until I happened in for lunch one day and made her an offer she couldn't refuse.'

His phone beeped then and Millie took his jacket as he excused himself and checked the caller ID. 'He did too,' Millie agreed conspiratorially, her smile growing dimples and her clear green eyes sparkling. 'And the next thing I knew, I'd upped sticks and was living on a tropical island paradise. Mind you, this one could talk the leg off a chair. So you watch out, Miss Turner, if you know what's good for you.'

'Now, Millie,' Daniel cautioned, sliding his phone away. 'Don't go giving away all my trade secrets.'

'Thanks for the advice,' Sophie told Millie, seeing a different side to Daniel and enjoying the unexpected banter between employer and employee. 'I'm not actually sure I'll be staying for dinner, but I'll definitely take all the tips I can get.'

Millie looked genuinely disappointed until Daniel intervened. 'Of course Miss Turner is staying for dinner,' he announced. 'And, in the meantime, I wonder if you might show her to the guest room and rustle up a swimsuit? I'll catch up in a while. I have a couple of calls to make.' And then he smiled. 'Just don't be too hard on her heels.'

'Of course. I know just the suit for you. Come this way.' Millie bustled up a short flight of timber stairs to another level and a long passageway. 'What was that about heels?' she asked, glancing over her shoulder.

'He was having a joke at my expense,' Sophie admitted. 'I thought I had to walk down to the beach for a swim and I used my shoes as an excuse. I didn't realise there was a pool.' She didn't admit she was trying to avoid swimming with Daniel full-stop, but if he was busy with calls maybe she could get in a quick dip now. She could surely do with a cool down to dispel some of this heat.

Millie chuckled. 'He has a way with him, that one. There is a path down, and the beach is just beautiful. Get Daniel to show you. But, yes, preferably when you're wearing flat shoes.'

Sophie smiled her thanks. As much as the beach looked special, she was sure she wouldn't be around long enough for a personal inspection.

But that didn't stop her appreciating the house itself with its high-ceilinged rooms, cool timber floors and a wall of windows that brought the magnificent view inside. 'It's always nice when Mr Caruana brings a friend home,' Millie offered as she led the way. 'I tell him it's not natural for one man to rattle around a big house like this all by himself. I keep telling him he has to settle down one day.'

The house was indeed enormous, wrapped around a hillside so you couldn't see from one end to the other—although why would you want to look anywhere but at the view, which changed with every angle, a view now complemented by the crystal-clear infinity pool that bordered the decking. An aqua plunge-pool lay at one point that a casual living-area wrapped around.

But Millie's words settled heavily on Sophie as she followed her into a bedroom that looked out over treetops to aquamarine waters and the mainland coast beyond. *Friend*. The housekeeper assumed she was Daniel's latest girlfriend. 'We're not actually friends. Not like that, I mean. I'm just waiting for Monica to call from Honolulu. I'm organising her wedding.'

'Monica's getting married?' The housekeeper abandoned her rummaging in the fitted wardrobe and turned around, delighted. 'Well, I never! That is exciting news. Who's the lucky man?'

'My brother, Jake, actually.'

Millie smiled broadly. 'Then you're much better than a friend. You're practically family.' She returned to the surprisingly well-stocked closet. 'Now, let's see, there's a colour in here that would suit you perfectly. Where is it?'

'Who owns all these clothes?' she said, looking around, wondering about the guest room with its high bed, snowy-white comforter and cupboard brimming with clothes.

'They're just spares, really. Handy in case Monica drops by with friends.'

Sophie could see Monica used the room sometimes. There were pictures of her on a dressing table. One of her in bathers at the beach. Another in school uniform, grinning self-consciously, trying not to show her braces. She smiled at that one. She remembered the ignominy of braces herself. Only for two years, but at the time it had seemed like an eternity of humiliation. And she'd resented it so much she'd never really thanked her mother for doing all those hours of overtime so she could afford to pay for them.

She put the photo down, lip stuck firmly between now perfectly aligned teeth. God, she missed her mum. Thank heavens Jake had found her after her death. It was one thing to be independent, rational and aloof, but it could be lonely.

There was another photo, but Sophie didn't recognise who it was. She picked up the silver frame. A pretty girl with laughing eyes looked out at her, her long blonde hair whipping around her face as she blew a kiss to the camera.

'Ah, here we are,' said Millie from behind her. 'Try this one for size, and there's a matching sarong. I'll fetch you a towel.'

Sophie turned, caught the gleam of sapphire-and-gold coloured fabric on the bed and smiled appreciatively. It was a rich, sumptuous pattern, and with a sarong to cover her she wouldn't feel quite so undressed. 'Thank you, Millie, it's lovely. By the way, who's this—do you know? One of Monica's friends? I don't think I've met her, although I've met the girls she's asked to be bridesmaids.'

Millie drew close and took the picture from her, giving the glass a gentle dust with a cloth she pulled from a pocket in her apron, her smile now sad. 'A good friend of Daniel, apparently. Died in tragic circumstances. Daniel can't bear to have the photograph where he can see it, but he can't bear to put it away, so it hides in here where he's unlikely to come across it. Pretty little thing, wasn't she? I sometimes wonder if…'

The woman trailed off to silence and Sophie wondered if it was because her thumping heart had drowned out the other woman's words. Why did it matter so much? She didn't know, but she had to ask. 'What do you wonder?'

Millie sighed. 'Oh, just whether whatever happened back then turned Daniel off the idea of ever getting attached to anyone else. Apparently it was quite serious.' Then she flicked her cloth over the shelf before she replaced the photo. 'Ah well; I best be getting you that towel.'

Sophie sat down on the side of the bed, idly picking up the richly coloured wrap the woman had left. The fabric slipped through her fingers, smooth and shimmering, a faint gold thread catching the light. Exquisite.

But then her eyes were drawn again to the picture of the smiling girl—so special to Daniel that he couldn't bear to look at her photograph, so special that he couldn't bear to part with it.

Had it been Daniel holding the camera all those years ago? Had the love shining in her eyes and that kiss been meant for him?

He must have loved her very much.

For some inexplicable reason she didn't want to linger too long on that thought. It was hard imagining Daniel loving anyone; he seemed so driven and angry and unrelenting, and if he'd ever had a heart it was so deeply buried it had probably atrophied by now. Even his love for his sister seemed more of a guard-dog mentality than brotherly love.

She scooped up the bikini and headed for the *en suite*. A swim was definitely what she needed right now. Given Daniel was busy with his calls, she'd have the pool to herself for a while. And when he did arrive she could plead she'd had enough and cover herself with the sarong.

Besides, Millie was here. What on earth could she have to worry about?

CHAPTER SEVEN

'WHAT have you got?'

'She's Fletcher's sister all right.' Jo's voice sounded like gravel rattling down the line. 'Seems her parents broke up and split the kids.'

Daniel leaned back and put his feet up on his desk. So it was as she'd said. He wasn't sure whether he was relieved she hadn't been lying, or disappointed she really was related to that Fletcher scum. 'And the business?'

'It exists. Small to middling. Seems to have a good reputation, although business has been a bit thin on the ground lately.' There was a weighted pause. 'Could definitely do with an injection of funds.'

Daniel's gut churned and he dropped his feet to the floor. 'You think she's after a cut?'

'What else would she be doing here? Monica's old enough now to take herself off and get married without your permission. This Miss Turner, or whatever she calls herself, is here to make the wedding look legit—nothing surer—so you'll panic and offer more for Fletcher to clear off.'

A growl rose in his throat. Yet she'd acted as if her brother's affair with Moni was the romance story of the decade. But Jo's discoveries had only confirmed what he'd first suspected as soon as she'd finally revealed who she was: she was in it for the money. Nothing more.

Which made her a superlative actress. But then, con men—and con women—usually were.

'We're talking to Monica tonight. Once I find out where they're staying, I want you to get an offer to him.'

Jo was well rehearsed in the drill, all except for the one variable. 'How much?'

Daniel had been mulling over the same thing himself. It wasn't going to be cheap, so there was no point starting low and extending the process with bid and counterbid. 'Let's cut to the chase. Offer him a million. The usual deal: clear off and never get in touch with Monica again.'

'A million? Jeez, boss, offer me a million and I'll never talk to Monica again myself.'

'Quit it, Jo!' he said, not in the mood for jokes. Besides, it wasn't as if he didn't pay his security manager a better than decent salary. He massaged his forehead with his fingers. 'This is serious.'

'I am serious,' the man protested, although this time the laughter was noticeably absent from his voice. 'You'd offer that bastard a million dollars when you know he's only going to ask for more? You know he's not worth it.'

'It's worth whatever it takes to get him away from Moni! You understand that?'

'Yeah. Of course, boss,' he said grudgingly. 'I was there, remember?'

Daniel remembered. Jo had been there through those years of high school to witness Fletcher's futile efforts to prove himself Daniel's equal over and over. The scholarship kid with a chip the size of a log on his shoulder versus the kid with money—not that his family had hung onto that long enough to enjoy it. But all those challenges, brawls and endless niggling irritations to prove he was as good as, if not better than, Daniel—Jo had been there. Jo had seen it all.

Fletcher had been a poster boy for persistence, and the ironic thing was that by the time the final year was over, Daniel had almost developed a grudging admiration for him. He'd felt the kid with the deadbeat father might actually make something of himself.

Or so he'd thought.

Until he got the phone call that changed his life.

The phone call telling him Emma was dead.

He'd realised then that Fletcher hadn't just wanted to be as good as Daniel Caruana. He'd wanted to *be* him, lock, stock and fiancée.

It was Jo who had scraped Daniel off the floor and stood by him while they'd buried the girl he'd loved. Jo who had fed him beer after beer while he spilled his guts about all the ways he was going to kill Fletcher. Jo who had convinced him Fletcher wasn't worth it and had stopped him when drunken bravado had convinced Daniel it was the only option he had.

Yeah, Jo had been there, and his loyalty deserved better. 'I know he'll ask for more,' Daniel continued, his tone less aggressive. 'He knows more than anyone what Moni's worth— but I bet Miss Turner will soon get him to agree, simply so she can get off the island and collect her cut.'

There was another pause. 'She's still there, then?'

'The fastest way to prove she's in on it is to force her to organise a wedding she knows isn't going to happen. She won't be able to keep up the pretence twenty-four hours a day.'

'You reckon she'll stay put, then?'

'She's not leaving the island. Not while Fletcher's got my sister.'

He severed the connection with an assurance he'd call with Moni's location as soon as he'd heard from Honolulu. Then he dropped his feet to the floor and swung his chair around to gaze out through the wall of windows, grateful that there was someone who understood, someone who knew the history, who didn't have to ask too many questions.

What would he do without Jo? His old high-school friend had also been there when one of Moni's first boyfriends had decided that she was worth more in cold hard cash than for herself. Barely eighteen, Monica had fallen head over heels, never realising that at the same time the guy was pretending to be the man of her dreams he was threatening to publish secret images of them on the Internet. Daniel's sister, immortalised on film, at what should be one of the most intimate and special times of her life. Unless her brother paid—big time.

Jo had arranged the payment to send him on his way and the bastard had disappeared, the files destroyed. But it seemed there was always someone else lining up to take his place, someone ready to accept an offer before they had time to do any damage.

Given they'd taken the money, didn't that prove that it was the dollars they'd really cared about?

Fletcher would be just the same—worse, really, given his history.

The sapphire perfection of sea and sky suddenly came into focus, filling his vision as he dragged in air, restoring him.

Jo wouldn't fail him. The trap would soon be set and Fletcher would soon be gone. And meanwhile...

A movement low down in the window snagged his attention, a ripple at the end of the pool.

He growled.

Meanwhile he had other things to attend to.

She might be a good actress, but she wasn't the only one who could play at make believe. Only, the way he played, she'd soon be wishing she'd never gone along with that deadbeat brother of hers.

He made another quick phone call, anxious now to join her in the pool, eager to take the game to the next level but first needing to make sure that she had no argument for a sudden departure.

Because Miss Turner wasn't going anywhere, any time soon.

Sophie rested her chin on her crossed arms on the edge of the pool and floated as she gazed out at the expanse of sea and sky. The warm air was sweet here, any hint of salt or beach concealed under the scent of the tropical flowers that clambered rampant over walls and gateways. It was paradise.

But she was here to do a job. She had to keep reminding herself of that, because instead of focusing on Jake and Monica's needs she found her thoughts more and more hijacked by the bride's brother.

How could she trust him, both after the way he'd treated her and had spoken of Jake this morning? How could she believe he was now so keen for this wedding to go ahead here, a wedding that he'd been so vehemently opposed to and probably still was, if truth be known?

And how could she trust herself if, knowing what she did, she still practically swooned every time his lips drew close? Was it wrong to be so aware of and so attracted to your potential brother-in-law?

Tiny birds darted through the whispering treetops, unconcerned by her presence, while brightly coloured butterflies negotiated a zig-zag course through the air, so close at times that she could almost reach out a hand and scoop them into her palm.

It had just been a kiss, she reminded herself for what must have been the hundredth time. Nothing more. And nothing would come of it, she knew. A man like Daniel would have a little black book the size of the phone book; given the unsurprised look on Millie's face when she'd been introduced, half of them had no doubt turned up here for a swim and who knew what else? A kiss would mean nothing to a man like him.

A few moments with the water lapping at her breasts gave rise to a new thought: maybe it did mean something? He was a businessman, used to tactics in the boardroom and no doubt in the bedroom. Was that latest kiss designed to throw her, to make her think he was interested, all in the hope of disarming her defences? Maybe he thought that if he seduced her he might drive a wedge between her and Jake? Divide and conquer—was that his ploy?

But if he seriously thought she could be seduced by a few kisses into doing his bidding he could think again. She kicked lazily at the water while she mulled over the thought, wondering if she could turn it to her advantage. She wasn't sure she knew enough to play the attraction game; she hadn't had near enough experience with men. But maybe, if he got to know her a little better, he might be more willing to listen to her, and maybe he might see that Jake wasn't all bad.

The sun felt warm on her shoulders and she slipped back to duck them under the water to cool them down. She'd get out soon, before Daniel finished with whatever business was keeping him. But it was too delicious not to enjoy just a minute longer.

Her feet swirled the water behind her, not enough to break the surface, just moving the water enough so that it swirled and eddied around her in a blissful water-massage, soaking away the tensions of the day. She sighed and closed her eyes. A person could get used to this. Just a minute more…

Something cold hit her back and she came to with a start. 'You'll burn if you're not careful.'

She would have jumped to her feet, but her arms were tangled, her thoughts already in havoc. Already he was there beside her, his feet planted in the water alongside and his hands on her shoulders, long fingers rubbing lotion into her skin, the press of his hand not allowing her up. 'You were asleep,' he said, clearly delighted with the discovery.

'I must have dozed off,' she said breathlessly. 'It was so relaxing.'

'You don't feel relaxed,' he bothered to note. 'You feel as stiff as a board.'

There was good reason for that, she thought wryly as his hand sought to work the lotion into her back with long, languorous strokes. Long strokes that transmitted their languid caress all the way down to her core and made her even tenser. She squeezed her eyes shut, wishing she could so easily block out the sensations assailing her. This was no casual application of sun block. This was a caress. Every one of his fingertips was like a probe that sought and found exactly the right pressure points to make her gasp with pleasure.

When he kneeled down in the water alongside her, his second hand joined the first, one hand at each shoulder, his fingertips brushing perilously close to her breasts as he circled to her underarms. She couldn't take any more.

She pushed up, turning her head to roll over. 'I should get out.' She almost wished she'd stayed right where she was, for now she could see him. Her mouth went dry. She was surrounded by water, had probably been soaking long enough to turn into a prune, but right at that moment her throat was drier than the Sahara in a sandstorm.

Because somehow she'd known he'd wear black, had known he'd wear it better than most against his sun-bronzed skin. But nowhere in her wild imaginings had she'd estimated he'd bypass simply being devastating and head into the realm of the gods of ancient mythology. He was way beyond dangerous. He was positively lethal.

'There's no rush, is there?'

Against her better judgement, his words made some kind of sense as she drank in the olive-skinned perfection of his torso, the whirls of dark hair dusting his naked chest, only to arrow down to his naval and disappear in a line in his trunks. Maybe he was right—there was no rush. So why her desperate rush to get away?

Oh yes...

'Monica might call,' she managed at last, levering the tongue from the roof of her mouth and peeling her eyes away to locate her sarong in the same action, mentally estimating the seconds before she could hide herself beneath it. 'I want to be ready.'

'She already called.'

Her eyes flicked back to his, sure she'd misheard. 'She what?'

'I just spoke to her. She couldn't raise you on your mobile so she checked with your office and they told her you might still be up here.'

Now he had her full attention, and not just because he had a body that shorted her senses. She rolled over until she was sitting up on the submerged ledge of the pool, thoughts of imminent escape momentarily forgotten. 'Monica called and you didn't bother to let me know? When you know I've been waiting for her call?'

'She did try to call you,' he reminded her. 'Is it my fault you didn't pick up? But does it really matter who she spoke to? The important thing is, she said she's delighted to have the wedding here on Kallista.'

'Oh, I'll just bet she did.' Sophie rose up like the proverbial phoenix, water sloughing from her limbs. For the first time she was uncaring at being clad in only a bikini, if only because she was so angry. 'Because you no doubt told her the Tropical Palms was now unavailable.' She swiped up the sarong from the chair where she'd left it and knotted it around

FREE BOOKS OFFER

To get you started, we'll send you
2 FREE books and a FREE gift

There's no catch, everything is **FREE**

Accepting your 2 **FREE** books and **FREE** mystery gift
places you under no obligation to buy anything.

Be part of the Mills & Boon® Book Club™ and receive your favourite
Series books up to 2 months before they are in the shops and delivered
straight to your door. Plus, enjoy a wide range of **EXCLUSIVE** benefits!

- Best new women's fiction – delivered right to
  your door with FREE P&P

- Avoid disappointment – get your books up to
  2 months before they are in the shops

- No contract – no obligation to buy

We hope that after receiving your free books you'll
want to remain a member. But the choice is yours.
So why not give us a go? You'll be glad you did!

Visit **millsandboon.co.uk** to stay up to date
with offers and to sign-up for our newsletter

2 **FREE** books
and a
FREE gift

P0HIA

Mrs/Miss/Ms/Mr   Initials _____

                                          BLOCK CAPITALS PLEASE

Surname _____

Address _____

_____

                         Postcode _____

Email _____

NO STAMP NEEDED!

MILLS & BOON®
Book Club

FREE BOOK OFFER
FREEPOST NAT 10298
RICHMOND
TW9 1BR

NO STAMP
NECESSARY
IF POSTED IN
THE U.K. OR N.I.

herself before searching for her phone, wondering how she could have missed a call. Even if she'd dozed off, it would have woken her.

'It is unavailable. I didn't realise it was a secret. You should have said.'

'And you should have called me!' she said, lifting her towel, knowing the phone had to be here somewhere. 'Monica might be your sister, but I'm supposed to be the one who's organising this wedding for her and Jake.' She turned back, temporarily giving up on the phone. 'Or did Jake jump up and down with excitement at the prospect of holding the wedding here too? Somehow I doubt it, given how much you two seem to get on.'

His lips were a grim line. 'He was down at Reception. I didn't speak to him.'

'So you thought you'd take advantage before I had a chance to discuss the options with them first.' And then she remembered—she'd been so busy thinking about that picture in the guest room, and so desperate to have her swim before Daniel emerged from his calls, that she'd completely forgotten to grab her phone from her bag. *Damn.*

'What options?' he challenged from the pool, leaning back on the edge, looking way too relaxed and reminding her again of how a crocodile looked before it launched its attack on unsuspecting prey. 'You haven't one other option and you know it.'

But it was Sophie who snapped, angry with him for being so high-handed, angry with herself for being so distracted by thinking about him that she would make such a stupid mistake. 'Did I even get a chance to look? No, because the great Daniel Caruana has decided his is the only option. End of argument. Tell me, does it ever get boring riding roughshod over people or do you get some kind of kick out of it?'

'What are you so angry about?' The once-calm pool exploded, the water bubbling as Daniel erupted from the pool. Water sluiced from his body, running in rivulets down his long, powerful legs, and for the first time she got the full visual impact of the man under the clothes. He could have been a marble statue come to life, some mythical god from the ancient world with his proportional perfection of tautly packed body, long limbs and beating, savage heart. Her own heart thumped loud as he strode purposefully towards her, but it was the potent look in his eyes that turned that thudding beat to fear.

'You are lucky you have a venue at all,' he snarled. 'But, rather than thank me for bailing you out of your problem, you prefer to rail against me as if I have done you some kind of injustice.'

She turned to go, unwilling to hear any more, knowing that his words were at least partly true. Kallista did offer a solution to her problem of a lack of venue, even if it did offer up a host of other problems into the deal.

But she just couldn't take any more. She'd felt the balance of power shifting, and control of this wedding slipping through her fingers, ever since she'd first arrived in Daniel Caruana's offices this morning with what should have been the upper hand. And she'd felt control over her own emotions slipping away just as completely, until she felt raw, bruised and ill-prepared for yet another confrontation.

Yet another defeat?

Or would it end in yet another kiss? But even that would be no victory. 'I don't have to listen to this.' But his hand stayed her forearm, his powerful flick wheeling her right back so that she crashed bodily against him, the shock momentarily winding her.

Another kind of shock had her gasping then, for nothing more than damp fabric—once warmed by sunshine, now warmed by body heat—lay between them where their bodies met from chest to knee.

He might just as well have flicked a switch inside her. Like a power surge she felt the burst of sensation, the contact of flesh against flesh generating a warmth that swelled her breasts and turned her nipples hard. At the same time it pooled and she felt aching heat low in her belly. When she breathed, even that tiny movement created a friction that ramped up the sensations tenfold. She couldn't even take a breath without breathing him in with it.

'What are you afraid of?' he demanded, his eyes searching her face. 'Why are you always so desperate to run away from me?'

'Who says I'm afraid?' But she belied her own defence with breathless words that sounded like she'd been turned upside down and shaken till they'd rattled from her.

He frowned, her trembling arm still held prisoner in his own. 'Am I really that terrifying?'

'I'm not…' Her teeth snagged her bottom lip. There was no point pretending she wasn't afraid, but she didn't have to admit it, either. She kicked up her chin. 'I'm not running now.'

The look in his eyes turned distinctly primal even as he smiled. 'Just as well, because there would be no point. When I want something, I usually get it, whether or not it's a moving target.'

In her fractured mind, his words made no sense at all. 'What are you talking about?'

'I want you, Sophie. I wanted you when you showed up in my office in a buttoned-up dress and with a buttoned-up attitude to match. I want you even more now I've seen you out of both of them.'

The shudder caught her unawares, like his words and she trembled openly against him. 'Daniel, I…'

He stroked her hair, catching a stray tendril and winding it around her ear, his touch tender, sensual and tingle-inducing. 'You feel it too,' he said, even as his gaze remained focused on the hand stroking her hair. 'You feel this attraction between us.'

She tried to tell herself it was all part of the plan. Tried to convince herself that this was what she had wanted, to get Daniel on side and ensure that he might be more receptive to ensuring the wedding between his sister and her brother would be a success.

But how could she pretend it was all part of a plan when she didn't have to pretend to sway into his touch? How could she make herself or anyone else believe it was otherwise? Then she felt his lips press against her hair, his warm breath against her scalp, and she was very nearly undone.

She swallowed against a need to lift her face and meet his lips with her own. Fought against it with all the power she could summon. But there was hardly any resistance left in her.

When he acted arrogantly and made all the decisions, when he was overbearing and unbearable with it, she could summon a resistance and fight him. But when he was like this—tender, gentle and with a touch that melted her bones and defused her resistance—how could she fight?

She couldn't.

Not when she knew he was right. Not when she knew she wanted him too. Damn it.

Sophie heard a knock and the sound of a door sliding behind her and she jerked away, but not as far as she'd have liked to because Daniel still kept hold of her arm. 'Excuse me for interrupting,' she heard Millie say, 'But Monica's on the phone again asking to speak to Miss Turner.'

It took a second for her brain to shift gears and to make sense of Millie's words. 'To me?' Daniel nodded.

'I didn't get a chance to tell you, but Moni said she'd call again once she'd had a chance to talk to Jake.'

Sophie didn't have to ask why he hadn't had a chance to say it—because she hadn't let him. She'd jumped straight down his throat and practically accused him of hijacking the wedding arrangements.

'I'm sorry,' she managed. 'I got the impression you were taking over.'

'So I gather.' He managed a tight smile. 'Maybe you'd better go take that call.' He nodded towards the door. 'Millie will show you to the office.'

'You're not coming?'

'Moni asked to speak to you. I thought you might appreciate doing it alone.' He watched her watching him for a second and then he said, 'Are you going to take the call or not?'

She nodded and disappeared into the house.

It was only a small lie, he told himself as he headed for his suite. He would normally go out of his way to be there, overseeing the call, ensuring it went in the right direction. But he'd planted the seed in Monica's mind and got her excited, and he was sure not even Fletcher could change her mind. She had no other option now. It was Kallista or nothing.

Besides, there was no way he was going to speak to Fletcher. He couldn't even bring himself to hear the man's voice.

If all went to plan, he would never have to. Once Jo contacted him and made him an offer, he'd be all too willing to escape a wedding planned slap-bang in the centre of the enemy camp. It shouldn't be long now, and they wouldn't see Fletcher for dust.

He snapped on his shower and waited for the steam to rise as he reefed off his swimming trunks, a niggling concern in the back of his mind.

Because there was another reason that had kept him from being there for that call. It was the smile he'd heard in Moni's voice when she'd talked about Fletcher, the admiration, the adoration.

Almost as if…

Almost as if she really was in love with him.

The thought nearly turned his stomach. No way, he thought, discarding the notion as he stepped under the cloudburst spray. She only thought she loved him. She was infatuated, like she always was, and probably on the rebound.

But if she did love him?

He breathed deeply, turning his face under the torrent. Then she would take the break-up harder than ever. He hated his own part in it, hated that he had to be the one to save her and yet maybe hurt her in the process. But who else could do it? Who else knew what Fletcher was capable of?

No, it was better to suffer now than for her to discover later that Fletcher had only ever been interested in her money.

And one day she would thank him, he was sure.

Monica was every bit as excited as Daniel had maintained. Getting married on Kallista was, in her words, a dream come true and she couldn't be happier. Then she handed the phone over to Jake so he could have a few words with his sister.

'What do you think, Jake?' Sophie asked. 'Are you happy about the change in venue?'

'Sounds like we haven't a choice, given the Tropical Palms has cancelled. But Monica's over-the-moon happy. And if Daniel can see his way clear to offer his island I don't see how I can say no.'

Which meant *she* couldn't say no. She dragged in air, suddenly hot, those places in her body that had so recently been pressed up against Daniel's hard, packed torso throbbing all over again. For Jake's agreement had sealed her fate—the island of Kallista would host the wedding and there was no getting out of it now, no escape from dealing with Daniel Caruana. But when had that concept secretly thrilled rather than repulsed her? And when had she started looking forward to seeing more of him, rather than less?

When he had set her body alight with just one look, just one touch? Or when he had told her that he wanted her?

'What does surprise me,' her brother continued, forcing her thoughts back to the phone call, 'is that he's being so supportive. I didn't expect that.'

He wasn't the only one. In one day she'd been witness to Daniel acting as if Jake was the devil incarnate who would never in a million years marry his sister, then offering his idyllic island as the venue for them to seal their vows. And here was Jake, more resigned than enthusiastic about the change; she knew he was going along with it because it was what his bride wanted.

'What happened between you two?' she asked. 'I'm beginning to hope Daniel might be coming around to the idea of his sister getting married, but something more than high-school competitiveness must have happened. His reaction this morning to the news was nothing less than extreme.'

There was a weary sigh at the end of the line and she suspected it wasn't all about jet lag. 'Look, Sophie, it's not something I really want to talk about over the phone. I'm not even sure I know the whole story myself. I was hoping I could clear the air with Daniel before we left but he wouldn't return my calls.'

'Maybe you should come back via Cairns, then, and sort it out before the wedding. Daniel might be more comfortable with the whole idea by then. It could be a good time to mend some bridges.'

'Maybe you're right. Hey, we've gotta go. We've got a surfing lesson booked.'

She was just saying her goodbyes when he said, 'Oh, hang on—Monica just wants to say something.'

There was a brief hesitation and then, 'Sophie? I just wanted to thank you so much for being there,' Monica said breathlessly, as if she'd made a sudden dive for the phone. 'Daniel told me you'd be staying on Kallista now until the wedding, to make sure everything is absolutely perfect. It means so much that you're prepared to do that. Thank you so much. See you when we get back!'

Monica was gone by the time Sophie could manage a numb reply and she replaced the receiver with more questions than answers. She was staying on Kallista?—Daniel had told Monica that? So when had he decided that was going to happen? And when had he been planning to fill her in on the details?

Her earlier apology for wrongly accusing him of taking control suddenly seemed premature. Daniel Caruana didn't just like things to go his way, he liked to be in the driver's seat to ensure he got where and what he wanted. It was like playing chess with someone who was always two moves ahead. There was no way she was going to be told what she was doing by him.

In the very next breath she remembered that it was Monica who had told her, Monica who had thanked her for staying. Sure, Daniel was clearly behind the idea, but Monica's effusive thanks for staying proved she was right behind the concept. Sophie was trapped somewhere between Daniel's heavy-handed tactics and her responsibility to Monica and Jake. Her very own rock and a hard place.

Infuriating man! But he was Monica's brother. He had to know his sister better than she did. After all, he'd been right about her wanting to get married on Kallista, hadn't he?

Maybe he really did just want his sister to be happy.

And then she almost laughed out loud. This was the man who'd made no apology for disposing of his sister's previous boyfriends by paying them to disappear. Instead he'd practically boasted about it! Was this a man who really cared about his sister's happiness? Not likely. Which brought her back to earth with a crash.

So why was he going along with these wedding plans?

Did he really believe his sister was in love this time? Given his mistrust of her previous suitors, and his intense dislike of her brother, the idea seemed incomprehensible. But what other reason was there for his suddenly being so compliant?

She didn't know. But what she did know was that this wedding would be everything that Monica and Jake wanted it to be, and that she would do her utmost to make it so—no matter what Daniel Caruana had planned.

CHAPTER EIGHT

DANIEL had been called away on an important call, Millie advised when Sophie emerged, but she was to show her to her new office and to make sure she had everything she needed in the guest room for her stay.

Sophie nodded numbly. Slowly she was coming to terms with the concept she might have to spend most, if not all, of the next few weeks here on Kallista if this wedding was to get off the ground. What was more disconcerting was that everyone else seemed to accept it as a given. It was just lucky Monica had warned her.

Clearly she could forget about getting back to Brisbane tonight, or any time soon.

'I didn't bring any clothes,' she offered by way of a half-hearted protest. Daniel had already taken care of that minor inconvenience, Millie informed her; a selection of items was arriving tomorrow to supplement whatever was already in the guest-room wardrobe.

Sophie suppressed her irritation. How typical of Mr Bossy Boots Caruana that now he assumed he could dress her. Did he think that just because he owned or employed everything and everyone on the island he now owned her too? Not a chance. She'd have Meg sort some stuff out and courier it up tomorrow. She might have to live here, but that didn't mean she'd have to wear his clothes.

The guest office sat at the far end of the house, just beyond her room, boasting a view that could never improve productivity, she was sure. The windows here were angled towards the mainland, the ribbon of white coast and lush green mountains the perfect foil for the cerulean perfection of sea and sky.

But, if you could manage to drag your eyes away from the view, the office had everything that opened and shut—computer, printer, wireless broadband along with a phone and fax.

Sophie looked around her, wondering at the calibre of person Daniel entertained here that he would have an entire guest office laid on, as well as a guest suite. Clearly not your average aunt and uncle. Not that she knew the first thing about his family, really, beyond the guest list Monica had provided her with.

In the space of a few short weeks she'd get to meet them herself, assuming she ever got the invitations out. Monica and Jake had decided on the stationery, but the printing had to wait until the venue was confirmed. That would be one of her first tasks, to get the invitations out; then, given the extremely short notice, she'd have to follow up each and every one by phone or email to ensure those who could make it would attend. Plus she'd have to add transfers to the arrangements too, she noted, for those arriving via Cairns airport. She'd ask Daniel about making available his helicopter, and maybe the launch he'd mentioned too.

The string quartet she'd organised could fly up, though she'd have to arrange flights and accommodation; then she had to find a cake, originally part of the Tropical Palms package. And Monica wanted doves.

She felt a rush of adrenaline as what seemed like a million thoughts vied for priority. This was what she loved about her job, the building blocks falling into place, the wedding becoming more real with every concrete decision.

This was only the tip of the iceberg. There was so little time and so much to do.

Game on.

Sophie surveyed the office around her and nodded approvingly. She'd need a space like this and it was good she'd be on the spot to iron out any difficulties as they arose. It made sense.

This wedding would be as perfect as she could make it, and Daniel would see he'd done the right thing by his sister and that he'd done the right thing by her. She was determined it would happen.

She looked up to see Millie waiting expectantly at the door. 'It's perfect,' she said with a smile, feeling good for the first time today. For she realised she was thinking about the wedding again, planning what had to happen. Doing her job instead of fantasising about the brother of the bride.

And didn't that make for a welcome change?

An hour later she'd showered and changed back into her own clothes and was in the new office, getting the computer set up with files from her USB drive, when Daniel knocked on the door. The look on his face was unreadable. 'Making yourself at home?'

In a cool linen shirt and lightweight trousers, he should have looked safer than the last time she'd seen him. Yet still his appearance sent a jolt to her senses and jagged her pulse a notch higher. Casual had never looked so sexy. Maybe it was the late o'clock shadow that graced his jaw that turned property magnate into pirate, but whatever it was it was a potent force that threatened to destabilise her and make her forget what she was doing here all over again.

'There's a lot to do, to get this wedding off the ground,' she managed. 'Especially given there's not much time.'

He cocked one eyebrow and tucked his hands into his pockets. 'I can imagine. Exactly why I knew it would be wise to base your operations here. I'm so glad you agree.'

She stood up straight. 'It's not about agreeing, though, is it? It's about making the best of it.'

But he just laughed off her thinly veiled objections and moved with that panther-like grace across the tiled floor to the wall of windows that lined one whole side of the room, gazing out over the beautiful view before he turned. 'I have to go to Townsville for a meeting early tomorrow and I'll probably be late back. Will you be all right by yourself?'

She was tempted to tell him that she'd get more done with him absent than with the distraction of him being around. But instead she said, 'I've got heaps to do. I doubt I'll even know you're gone.'

She could swear she saw a tic in his jaw as he looked her over; maybe he was just unimpressed she'd put her own dress back on rather than having chosen something from the wardrobe.

'I've arranged for a boutique to send clothes.'

She waved his offer away, his words confirming her suspicions. 'Thanks, but my assistant's sorting some clothes.'

'There's no need.'

'On the contrary,' she said firmly, 'There's *every* need, so long as they'll find a way over to the island. I'm having them couriered to your office.'

He nodded. 'They'll come over on the launch, then. I'll have the chopper in Townsville.'

'I need to talk to you about that,' she said, remembering one of the points on her to-do list. 'I'll have to arrange for transfers of guests from Cairns to the island. Will your helicopter be available for those? Or maybe the launch? Otherwise I'll have to try to secure another vessel.'

He pulled his hands from his pockets, looking suddenly uncomfortable, his eyes hooded as he checked his watch. 'Sure, make whatever arrangements you like. I forgot, Millie asked me to let you know dinner is ready. We're eating out on the deck. This way.'

She blinked in his wake, following him when it was clear he wasn't about to wait. So, now he'd guaranteed the wedding would be held here, she could do whatever she liked? She really didn't understand Daniel Caruana at all.

Late the next day Sophie put the phone down and rubbed the back of her neck, ready for a break, surprised to find it was already five o'clock. It had been a full-on day of organising, and she'd been on the phone since breakfast. It was amazing, she mused, just how much you could get done without distractions. Away from her own office, where the phone seemed to ring every ten minutes, and with Daniel away, she'd made amazing progress. Maybe this arrangement would work better than she'd expected. Millie popped her head around the door to tell her that dinner would be ready in an hour, which suddenly seemed an eternity away. Already the smells wafting their way from the kitchen had her stomach rumbling in anticipation. But then she had skipped lunch while she'd been on a roll.

What she needed first, though, was some exercise. A walk down those steps and a swim in the tiny cove would be perfect.

She changed into the blue bikini and dug out a pair of sandals from the bottom of the wardrobe that were more or less the right size. With a quick word to Millie to let her know where she'd be, she set off for the path. The steps down to the shore were longer and steeper than they looked and it took some time to wend her way down the short flight of steps that zig-zagged down the hillside. But she did keep stopping to enjoy the way the view changed from different angles. It was quiet here, peaceful; the rustle of lizards scurrying through the leaf litter, the call of birds and the gentle shush of sea meeting sand at the beach below was the music that accompanied her steps. The canopy sheltered the steps from the worst of the sun, but it was warm and still, and by the time she reached the white sand beach she did no more than kick off her borrowed sandals and untie her sarong before heading straight for the water.

Bliss. She sank down, letting the current play out her hair, letting the water refresh her. It was magic. Nobody could see her, nobody could bother her. It was like having her own private beach.

Oh yes. There were definitely compensations for having to stay on Kallista for a few weeks. The climb back was definitely the exercise she needed, and Sophie arrived breathless, hot but definitely more relaxed for the exercise. She patted her forehead with her towel as she slid open the door to her room, only to find someone already there.

'Well well, look what the cat dragged in.'

The man was on the other side of her bed, the side where she knew she'd left her handbag. He straightened and she got the impression of bulk and power; his arms were muscled, his hands curling and uncurling at his sides. A thief, here on Kallista? Daniel had said there were none. But it was the look in his eyes, the long, leery stare from top to toe, that made her shiver and suddenly feel fearful for Millie. Where was she? How had he got past her? 'Who are you?'

'So you're Fletcher's sister?'

She bristled, pulling the knot in her sarong tighter, the scent of stale cigarette-smoke hitting her nostrils. She didn't appreciate being so clearly at a disadvantage, and had no intention of answering his question if he wouldn't answer hers. 'What are you doing in my room?'

'I have to admit, I didn't expect you to be such a good looker.'

Sophie tried to look past him—surely Millie was around somewhere?—but his shoulders were so broad he blocked her vision of the door. 'I wish I could return the compliment, but as I didn't expect you at all, Mr…?'

'Call me Jo. I'm Caruana's security manager. Just checking to make sure everything's all right for the little lady.'

Snooping, more like it. At Daniel's behest? Then he smiled and took a step closer, holding out his hand, a big, beefy paw with a brassy gold watch at his wrist, a thick, gold chain that matched the one at his neck. Two gold bands glistened on nicotine-stained fingers. Reluctantly she put her own hand out, felt it practically absorbed into his and had to stop herself from pulling away.

'A pleasure to meet you.' She wondered if she'd misjudged him. He was large framed, but it was all muscle, like you'd expect on someone who worked in security, and when he smiled he didn't look quite so frightening. But then his eyes shot a glance down her body, lingering where she knew the two sides of the sarong parted near her bikini bottoms. 'All of you, that is.' She decided she didn't like the man after all.

'Is that you back, then?' Millie's voice sounded down the hallway and Jo dropped her hand and turned.

'Hello, Millie. Just getting acquainted with our new guest.'

'Oh, Jo,' she said, wiping her hands on her pinny as she looked uncertainly from one to the other. 'I didn't know you were here.'

'I didn't want to disturb you, Millie. I let myself in.'

The older woman sniffed, as if he should know better than go skulking around the house by himself, but she said nothing more to him. 'Dinner's almost ready, lovey,' she told Sophie. 'If you want to get out of your wet things.'

'Sounds good, Millie,' Jo said. 'I've missed your cooking at the café.'

'Won't your wife be expecting you?'

'Not tonight. She's staying at her sister's. And I did go to all the trouble of bringing this…' He reached down and picked something from the floor then placed it on the bed. A parcel. Sophie could see by the return address that it had come from Meg.

'My clothes?'

'I thought you might be needing this sooner rather than later.'

'Thank you.' So he hadn't been snooping. Or had he just taken the opportunity for a little digging while he was making the trip?

Jo sucked in air and gave another self-satisfied grin. 'I reckon I might have earned myself a dinner. What do you reckon?'

She looked searchingly at Millie. She didn't relish the idea of sharing a meal with someone who made her feel so ill at ease, but would it be churlish to refuse, given he'd brought her clothes? Was it her decision to make?

'Where is everyone?' Daniel's voice boomed down the hallway and she wanted to sag with relief. He was back earlier than expected and she wanted to hug him. If Jo stayed to share dinner, she'd feel much better if Daniel was that too—even though Daniel was as dangerous as hell and made her feel at times as skittery as a cat on a hot tin roof. Much safer.

He entered the room and took in the scene, smiling at Millie. He scowled, she realised, when his gaze fell on her, still damp from her swim. 'Jo,' he said, jerking his eyes to the big man. 'I didn't expect to see you here.'

His security chief crossed to his boss. 'I just dropped off that package you said might turn up.' He hesitated a fraction or two. 'You were going to be longer in Townsville, I thought.'

One half of Daniel's mouth turned up. 'We finished up early. Thanks for delivering the package. Did you have anything else for me?' The big man shook his head.

'I'm waiting. I'll text you.'

Daniel nodded. 'Then if that's all?'

'Well, all except for Friday night's poker game—we still on for that?'

Daniel looked at Sophie, a frown tugging his brows. 'Not this week. Maybe next.'

Jo followed his gaze and smirked. Sophie wanted to protest that it was nothing to do with her, but he was already leaving. 'Later,' he said.

Millie gave a matter-of-fact harrumph and excused herself for the kitchen with the news that dinner was now only ten minutes away.

Daniel leaned one hand against the wall and sighed. Sophie sure was a sight for sore eyes. Her hair was wild and stiff around her face, her damp sarong clinging to every curve, and he applauded the disarray. She looked so much better like this than in that buttoned-up dress he'd seen her in yesterday. She looked more real. More woman. Oh yes; coming home early was the best decision he'd made in a long while.

She looked in the direction where Jo had exited. 'I don't think I like that man.'

'Jo? Why? What did he do?'

'He was just…' She crossed her arms over her chest and shivered. 'I don't know. Creepy—the way he looked at me.'

'Jo's ex-army. He's tough, but he's a good operator. One of my most loyal employees, in fact.' Still he noticed the tremor that moved through her, and he wondered if there was more to it than she was letting on. Then again, no man in his right mind wouldn't want to stare at Sophie, given the way she looked right now, still damp from the sea, her cheeks flushed, her hair like he imagined it would look after a long, hot session making love.

Damn. Come to think of it, he wasn't sure he liked the idea of anyone else wanting to stare, not if their thoughts ended up along the same path...

He had to change the subject. 'How was your day?'

She blinked, and once again he got to appreciate that sweep of impressive lashes against her cheek. Strange, how something so innocent could be so sexy.

'I got a lot done.'

He smiled. He'd just bet she had; probably lazed around the pool all day. 'Because I wasn't here?'

'It helped.'

Her honest reply made his smile grow wider. He'd been right to ditch that meeting early. Debate had been going round and round for hours; ordinarily he would have stopped it long before. Whereas she maintained she'd found his absence productive, he'd been distracted all day by thoughts of her, what she was doing in his house, and whether she was wearing that blue bikini again.

How much more enjoyable to be here, at home, and see that she was.

'Are you hungry?'

He could swear he saw something in her eyes flare. Desire? He wanted to think so. For he was hungry for more than just food now and it would suit him fine if she felt the same way. There would not be that many opportunities, not once the offer process got under way and Fletcher's plan started to unravel. It would be foolish to waste the few nights they had.

'Famished,' came her softly spoken response through lips plump and pink—tastier than anything Millie might serve up, he knew. For a moment, he was tempted to dip his head and taste her once again and forget all about dinner. But instead he merely took her hand, ignoring her protest that she needed to shower when she looked ready to serve up on a platter herself.

'Then we should eat.'

He liked watching her eat, he decided through the meal as twilight moved to dark within minutes. He liked watching her, full-stop. Even when she was talking incessantly about the wedding and the arrangements she'd apparently made, as if he was actually interested, he liked watching her. Her face was animated, her eyes bright, whether gilded by the lowering sun's rays or, like now, kissed by the soft pearlescence of the moon; that was all that mattered.

She was beautiful.

She was here.

And tonight he would have her.

Millie was serving up dessert when Sophie finally worked up the courage to ask; he'd glossed over her questions about the guest list earlier. In fact, he'd glossed over anything to do with the wedding, with glib responses that had given her nothing. But if she was going to get these invitations out this week it would help to understand something of Monica's family. Besides, she was curious. And, given Daniel seemed to be in a good mood tonight, there was no time like the present.

'Your family name is Italian,' she said, 'But you were born here, weren't you? I know Monica was. Was it your parents who came from Italy?'

He took a sip of his coffee before leaning back in his chair and lacing his fingers in his lap. A delaying tactic, she knew, because the coffee was still way too hot to drink. For a while she wondered if he was going to answer her question at all.

'No,' he said at last. 'It was my grandfather who came out. He was barely out of his twenties, and desperate to work anywhere. He landed a job on a tobacco farm up at Mareeba.' He pointed to the dark shadow of mountains that loomed above the line of lights along the coast, marking the start of the hinterland. 'It's an hour or so up from Cairns on the Atherton Tablelands. He worked hard, and in a few years he'd earned enough to buy his own place. Married the daughter of another tobacco-farming family and was probably planning on starting a dynasty. Didn't work out that way. My father happened along late, and they never had any more kids.'

She nodded. So he'd grown up without uncles, aunts and cousins, with the extended family back in Italy? That kind of explained why the guest list was short on family.

'Did your father take over the farm?'

'For a while, until he decided that sugar was the way to go and made the switch. He did all right, too, until the bottom dropped out of the sugar market. He made a few bad decisions and was wiped out.'

'Oh, but I assumed…'

He smiled. 'That I was born with a silver spoon in my mouth? I was. Only to have it wrenched out when I was barely out of high school. My dad never got over the loss. He felt like he'd betrayed his father's trust and let my mother down. He was never the same after that.'

He was staring at his hands and she knew he was thinking about his parents; Sophie didn't have to ask. Monica had spoken of the car being swept from the road into a swollen creek in the midst of near-cyclonic conditions. She'd told her about the police arriving at the house to give them the grim news that their parents were never coming home. She'd told her how Daniel had held her while she'd cried that night, and every night for a week, and told her he'd never let anything bad happen to her.

No wonder he was so protective of his little sister.

She was the only family he had.

Strange, how she'd divorced that story from her first impressions of Daniel. It didn't fit the picture she'd had in her mind of the arrogant businessman who got his own way whichever way he could. But it was this man, sitting beside her, who'd cradled his grieving sister in his arms and tried to soothe away her tears. It was this man who'd practically raised her.

'Your parents would be proud of you with all you've achieved.'

He scoffed. 'Well, when you've lived in luxury, you know what you're missing when you've not got it. It's a powerful motivator.'

'I'm sure there's more to it than that. You did it the hard way. You had to drop out of university to look after Monica.'

He shrugged. 'Maybe. I got lucky, too. I stumbled into a job in a property-management business and it was a good fit. The property market was just starting to take off when I started dabbling. It paid off.'

Coming from one of Queensland's richest men, it was a massive understatement.

He downed his cooling coffee in one long gulp and stood. 'This is boring.'

She pushed back her own chair, her cheeks burning with embarrassment. 'I'm sorry. Dinner was wonderful, thank you. But I should leave you now.'

He was at her side in a heartbeat, his hand curled around her neck. 'I don't want you to leave me. I just don't want to talk about me.'

'What would you rather talk about?'

'Who said anything about talking?'

CHAPTER NINE

SHE would have laughed. She wanted to laugh, to dispel the tension that had suddenly weighted down the air until it was heavy and thick with anticipation. But the look in his eyes told her it was no accident.

'All night,' he whispered, his eyes on her mouth, his other hand joining the first behind her neck. 'All that time we were sitting here, this is really what I wanted to taste.'

He dipped his head, his mouth brushing hers, his tongue flicking over her lips. 'Mmm, salt,' he said, licking her taste from his lips.

'I was swimming,' she said. 'At the beach.'

'I like it,' he said, already making another pass. 'And coffee, and something sweet.'

His kisses grew deeper, his lips coaxing hers apart, his tongue tasting her, exploring, inviting her into the dance.

The breeze whispered through the leaves, a bird called out its final goodnight and the moon hung low and turned the sea into a silver ribbon. But none of it mattered. Not now, not with his lips upon hers, his taste in her mouth and the feel of his hard body pressed up against her.

He was unrelenting; his kisses intensified. He ravaged her mouth, plundered its depths with his tongue and tipped her head back so he could turn his hot mouth to her throat until she was gasping with the heat, the pleasure and the need.

And when he took one breast in one hand her knees went weak.

'Make love to me,' he said as he nuzzled her ear. A wave of pleasure rolled through her, so intense and so huge that she thought it might carry her away. Instead it passed, leaving her skin alive and tingling and with a heavy pooling heat between her thighs.

'We barely know each other,' she whispered, amazed and impressed that with a body screaming 'yes' she'd managed to find at least some kind of defence. *Not that she'd actually said no.*

She didn't do casual sex; she didn't do one-night stands. She didn't need any man. And yet 'we barely know each other' was the best she could do?

'We know that we want each other.'

Unfair! Then she gasped, her protest forgotten as his thumb stroked a nipple, sending arrows of exquisite pleasure straight to her core. 'You want me.' It was true, but surely that wasn't the only point?

'I can't,' she said, shaking her head, finding him harder to shake. 'This is crazy. Jake and Monica…'

'Are in Hawaii.' His lips found hers again. Coaxing. Persuading.

She pulled away. 'But I'm supposed to be here planning their wedding.'

His hand kept her head close to his mouth even while she voiced her argument, returning to her lips as soon as she'd uttered her words. 'And meanwhile,' he asked, 'you should live like a nun?'

'But it doesn't mean anything.'

'It means we want each other.'

'I don't do this sort of thing.'

'Have you ever wanted to before?'

She shook her head, her teeth troubling lips already exquisitely sensitised as he took her head between his hands and looked at her. 'Then maybe it's time you did.'

She was drowning in his eyes, falling hopelessly and helplessly in the direction she knew she should not go. And there was nothing, no will or thought or crumb of hope to save her.

Except for…

'Millie!' she whispered, looking around, stiffening in his arms as she suddenly remembered where they were.

'Has taken herself off to her apartment for the night. We're alone, Sophie. Just you, me and the moon.' His hands skimmed down her back, collecting up the hem of her sarong and easing it upwards, his hands curving around her behind, skimming over the small of her back as his mouth continued to weave magic on hers. Grit rolled under his fingertips, and she flinched as she remembered the forgotten shower.

'This is crazy. I'm covered in sand.'

His face drew back, just enough so he could rest his forehead on hers and look into her eyes. 'Something that is easily remedied.' And she felt herself swept from her feet and into his arms as if she weighed nothing.

He moved with the certainty of a man who knew what he wanted, but beyond that with the certainty of a man who knew what she wanted too. She *did* want this. It might be crazy; it might be a type of madness. He eased open a sliding door with a foot, kissing her until she felt faint, breathless and giddy with desire.

It *had* to be madness, she told herself. One short day ago she couldn't wait to get away from this man, had sought to flee from his dangerous acquaintance, and yet now she was trembling at the prospect of making love with him.

No wonder she'd felt compelled to run. For even then, underlying the hostile emotions and bitter words of yesterday's torrid meeting, she'd sensed he'd connected with her on some deep, elemental level. A level she'd shied away from. A level she'd feared to explore.

It was too late for fear now, as he pushed open a door and kicked it shut with his foot. His room, she figured. It was wide and high and with a bed the size of a minor principality. He didn't bother with the lights. The silvery glow from the moon slanting through the windows was enough to light his way past the bed, where he lingered only long enough to kick off his sandals and rid himself of his phone, before heading to the generous *en suite* turned magical by the same warm lunar glow.

Still he kept her in his arms, even when he entered the spacious shower cubicle, even as he turned the taps on full.

She gasped as the first burst of water hit, the torrent from a showerhead the size of a dinner plate cool against her super-heated flesh. Then her vision and her senses cleared enough for her to realise the insanity of what he'd done. 'You're drenched!' But he only laughed and, keeping her so close to him that she could not miss the press of his arousal, lowered her slowly to the floor.

'Does it matter if they're wet when they're coming off anyway?'

His kiss was deep and filled with longing, filled with need, and she drank him in as the water poured around them, as he untied the knot of the sarong at her chest. The sodden fabric fell to the floor with a smack and she trembled, feeling exposed in just her bikini. 'You're beautiful,' he said as he looked at her, his eyes dark with desire, his hands skimming her sides, drinking in her curves. She trembled again because being exposed when someone she wanted wanted her suddenly felt good.

But not half as good as he felt.

The wet shirt clung to his skin, moulded to his shape, but it wasn't damp cotton she wanted under her fingertips right now, it was the skin he'd worn last night in the pool. The skin he'd held next to her when she'd tried to run away. She wasn't trying to run away now. This time all bets were off. She wanted that skin under her fingers. She wanted it next to her own.

She fumbled with a button as his mouth fused once more with hers, but her hands were trembling with need, the buttonhole was waterlogged and resistant, and fine motor-skills eluded her. The next button proved equally uncooperative, and with a burst of frustration she wrenched the sides of his shirt apart and his glorious chest was hers to explore. Her nails raked over his skin, her fingers relishing the feel of his hard, packed flesh and the tight nub of nipple.

He growled with approval into her mouth and let her go long enough to peel the shredded garment from his shoulders. Then he was back, his fingers busy at her back until she felt the strap of her bikini-top go.

He paused then, his hands at her sides, his brow upon hers, almost as if he was catching his breath. Then his hands scooped around and pushed the bikini top up from below, his hands capturing her breasts, his thumbs rolling her nipples so that she arched into his hands. Then he peeled the top over her head and kissed a hot path to her breast, and she wanted to sag when he drew her nipple in deep.

Something shorted inside her. She was sure she must have blacked out in that instant, in that moment of utter pleasure that had consumed her world. But then she was back, to find him performing equivalent magic on her other breast.

Oh God. Suddenly his shoulders and chest were not enough for her hands. She fought with his belt, wanting to release the bucking power she felt straining beneath, the power she ached to feel. The power she knew was intended for her.

Desperation ruled her actions as the water rained down, beating against her sensitised skin, pulsing down in time with her heartbeat—washing away the salt of her swim but, more than that, washing away the last of her inhibitions.

When had she become a woman who initiated anything sexually? she pondered vaguely as his mouth left her breasts long enough for her to wonder. When had she decided for once to embrace the dangerous, instead of the safe and solid path? His mouth moved south down her belly, his tongue circling her naval before darting inside, hot, hard and insistent, his fingers tugging at her bikini bottoms; she forgot how to think, only how to feel.

He pressed her against the tiled wall, one hand at her breast, the other at her thigh. His mouth—oh God!—his mouth was there, hot, wet and urgent, parting her and finding that slick, sweet spot that ached with primal need.

Her hands tangled in his hair as his tongue flicked a fiery trail around that tight nub of nerve endings; his fingers circled her very core and the sweet, perfect agony of expectation was almost so much that she cried out with the injustice of it all. Then he sensed her need and sucked her tight into his mouth, his fingers plunging deep inside her.

She came in an explosion of sensation and a rainbow of colours, vivid colours, she recognised vaguely as they splashed around her. Colours bright and beautiful, the colours of the tropics. Vivid, potent and alive.

The colour of Daniel.

He scooped what was left of her into his arms before she sagged to the floor, then he snapped off the tap and snatched up a towel in his fingers, splaying it out on the bed next door before he put her down on it.

'Wow,' she said, her senses still humming. 'Amazing.'

Her words were enough to make his erection buck under the sodden trousers she'd never quite managed to get off. The sight of her on his bed with the moonlight turning her skin pearlescent was another thing altogether.

God, he wanted her! She'd come apart so spectacularly it had been all he could do to resist lunging into her to share the moment.

But there would be other moments—as many other moments as he could manage before she discovered the truth.

He finished the job she'd started and unzipped his trousers, letting the weight of the water drag them to the floor, stepping out of them as he freed his aching self from the band of his underwear.

'*You're* amazing,' she said, her eyes wide, her voice a blend of awe and wonder.

He knelt on one knee beside her, coiling one finger through her damp hair, taking a corner of the plush towel and gently blotting away the droplets of water that beaded on her satin skin. 'It's you who are amazing,' he said, leaning over, his lips unable to resist the kiss-plumped allure of hers. 'And I want to be inside you next time you come.'

She looked up at him, her dark lashes blinking against her cheeks, and smiled. 'I want you inside me.'

He groaned, her words ratcheting up his desire and his need. He'd been at the razor's edge of release before, gratified beyond anything he'd known before at the power of the orgasm he'd driven her to with his mouth. But nothing would beat the heady sensation of being, and coming, inside her.

Their eyes caught, their mouths meshed and their bodies tangled on the bed, mouth to mouth, mouth to nipple, hand to naked flesh.

He groaned with pleasure as her fingers coaxed him, teased him, led him to her entrance.

Then she gasped as he found that place, and bucked involuntarily beneath him as he settled himself between her legs.

His body pulsed at her core; her body was already willing him deeper, but as much as he wanted her, somehow he still had the sense to drag a foil from the bedside table.

'Let me,' she said, her eyes shy, her long lashes sweeping her cheek as if she was too embarrassed to look at him. He realised what courage she possessed to ask that even as he handed it over. For this was not a woman who moved with practised ease. This was a woman out of her depth, caught in deep water and eager to learn how to swim. He groaned through teeth clenched tight as she rolled protection down his length; even while her look of concentration at doing the job right was almost endearing, he knew that her innocent handling might just be his undoing.

All of it was his undoing: the touch of her fingers. The invitation of her parted legs as she lowered herself back down. The heady scent of desire from a woman whose skin turned to pearl in the silvery lunar glow.

He held himself poised over her, a moment of calm before the storm, a moment to savour, a brief moment to wonder what he had done to deserve such a feast for the senses.

'Please!' she said, desperate now, driven, and prepared to beg as her body once again screamed for release that only he could give. 'Now, please!'

And he lunged inside her in one fluid stroke that buried him to the hilt. Her head dug deep into the bed, her eyes wide with wonder, her gasp strangled before it was given birth.

He could stay there, he decided, held hostage by those exquisite, tight walls for ever, and it would not be long enough.

But he could no more stay still than hold the moon captive to glow on her skin for ever. He eased himself back, felt rather than heard her tiny whimper of loss, and made up for it one-thousand-fold as he lunged home again. This time she did cry out and he captured her ecstasy in his mouth, tasting her pleasure as he built the rhythm of their joining.

She matched him, tilting her hips to change the angle, using her muscles to hold him just a moment longer even as the pace turned frenetic and uncontrolled.

Skin slick with sweat, she glowed in the moonlight as she writhed under him, her breathing erratic, her increasingly desperate cries torn from her as he plunged again and again into her depths.

'Daniel!' she cried, reaching for him blindly, teetering on the edge of the precipice they both shared. He drew one perfect breast into his mouth and sucked on it hard, ramming himself home and exploding inside her with what felt like fireworks.

She came all around him, a vivid starburst of colour and passion, a wild release that blew his mind and took him shuddering over the edge with her.

Later, when the silvery moon had tracked higher in the night sky and Sophie lay sleeping, he stood outside on the deck in a pair of shorts, his hands palm-down on the railing, his restless thoughts a dark hole in a world of such moonlit perfection.

Electric—it was the only way he could describe how she'd felt, like a switch had been thrown and she'd turned from woman into electrical storm, sparking, pulsing with energy, crashing like lightning about him.

But how many nights would they have? How many opportunities to sink himself into her exquisite depths and feel her body come apart around him?

He turned and looked through the windows of his room, to where he could make out her shape on his bed, her face turned away, one arm hanging over the side of the bed and a glorious curve of flesh from waist to hip illuminated by the pale moonlight.

How many nights?

Or was this thing to end before it began?

He walked barefoot along the deck, the rustle of leaves and the occasional rustle in the undergrowth the only sounds as he put off the inevitable, refusing to open the phone he'd heard beep—the reason he'd come outside.

Damn. He wanted Fletcher gone. He wanted this farce of a wedding to be proved the lie it was. But once it was, once Fletcher had his money, she'd be gone too, eager for her cut.

And by now Jo would already have made him an offer. Fletcher might already have said yes and be on his way back to collect it, setting Monica free.

He wanted Monica free.

But then Sophie would leave.

He rubbed the back of his neck and sighed. There was only one way to find out. He slid the phone open and clicked through to 'messages'.

It was from Jo.

With a tight gut he clicked it open, read the words—*Fletcher said no*—and released a lungful of air he hadn't realised he'd been holding.

He slid the phone shut and turned back to the shadowed view of diamond-crusted velvet sea and the clusters of lights along the coast. Jo would be waiting for his instruction to up the offer, but for the moment Jo could wait. Which meant that, for the moment, Sophie was his to enjoy.

Besides, she seemed to enjoy making her wedding plans— in fact, she'd seemed so full of it tonight that anyone would think *she* believed it was real.

Who was he to deprive her of her fun?

'Daniel?' She was standing half-behind the sliding door, wearing only the moonlight and a tumble of golden hair. Instantly he stirred to life. 'Is something wrong?'

He held out a hand to her. 'I couldn't sleep.' And sheepishly, like a shy virgin instead of a woman with the body and responsiveness of a goddess, she moved silently to join him, the sway of her breasts like a call to action.

She took his hand and allowed herself to be drawn into the circle of his arms at the railing. 'Is there anything I can do?' she asked as he nuzzled her neck from behind, breathing in woman spiced with the heady scent of their love-making; his hands traversed from breast to thigh in one delicious, sensual exploration that had her arching her back on a sigh.

Was there anything she could do?

Oh, sweet Jesus, yes.

She moaned as he parted her, sliding his fingers between her slick folds while he patted his pockets with his other hand; he wanted to howl at the moon when he found what he needed. 'Maybe there is something,' he groaned as he ripped open the packet with his teeth. He dropped his shorts and kicked them away as he donned protection, thankful when he had two hands free again to stroke her, two hands to both give and find pleasure.

'Daniel!' she cried, already panting, her nipples tight and hard between his fingers. The curve of her behind fitted his hand perfectly as he soothed her legs apart, entering her in one delicious thrust that had them both gasping.

The lights of the coastal towns winked on the distant shore, the sea glittered where kissed by the moon, and the warm breeze carried the perfume of a thousand exotic flowers. When they came, the lights, sea and moon stayed the same, but the warm, perfumed breeze carried with it the cry of both their names.

CHAPTER TEN

'NO RUSH,' Daniel said from behind his office desk. 'Let him sweat a little. We don't have to look too eager.'

Jo squirmed noticeably in his chair. 'I thought you were in a hurry.'

Daniel picked up a paperweight from his desk, testing its weight in his hands, thinking abstractly that Sophie's breasts must weigh about the same—only they filled his hands so much more satisfactorily.

'You *were* in a hurry, you said.'

'I hear patience is a virtue.'

Jo wiped his brow with a handkerchief. 'I think you should make him another offer. Ramp up the pressure. It's obviously what he's waiting for.'

'And I think you should listen when I say I'm happy to sit tight.'

'So you're not worried about your sister—with him—any more, then? After what happened to that other girl?'

Daniel dropped the paperweight back on the desk, swivelling his chair around to directly face the big man down. 'That *other girl's* name was Emma.'

'Yeah. Her. You wouldn't want the same thing to happen to Monica.'

Daniel was caught between a bloodlust for retribution for what had happened so many years ago, and an anger for what he stood to lose now. Who did Jo think he was, telling Daniel what was important?

But Monica was his sister.

And if anything happened to her, he would never forgive himself.

Whereas Sophie was a passing lust—entertaining; sexually satisfying; mind-blowing, even. But ultimately disposable.

They all were.

Unlike Monica. What right did he have to indulge his own primal urges before ensuring the safety of his own sister? 'All right,' he said through gritted teeth, seeing the sense in Jo's argument, glad he had someone who knew enough history to keep him honest. 'Double the offer. Make it two million.'

If Millie noticed or disapproved of the change in sleeping arrangements, she didn't say anything. And she must have noticed. Sophie's bed had been untouched whereas Daniel's bed was a total shambles with wet clothes trailing from the shower to the bed, even though she'd tried to minimise the damage. There was no way Daniel's housekeeper could miss the carnage or fail to extrapolate from it the facts.

Yet Millie's smile appeared genuine when she brought Sophie a cup of lemon-scented tea halfway through the morning. 'How's it going, lovey?' she asked, peering over Sophie's shoulder at pictures of wedding cakes she had pulled from the Internet. 'Ooh, aren't they lovely? I used to dabble with wedding cakes—nothing like these modern ones, of course— before I got work in the café.'

Sophie nodded absently. It was the full and pitiful extent of her work this morning, she reflected, this thin pile of pictures. She'd convinced herself it was work, even though she'd found nothing that nearly approximated the traditional and simple tiered cake Monica had hinted at—like the cake her parents had had at their wedding—even though her mind had been miles away.

Or, rather, hours ago.

If last night had blown away her every inhibition, this morning's efforts had blown her mind. Daniel was the kind of lover you only read about in books. Nobody could make love that many times in one night, she'd been convinced. Nobody.

But Daniel had. And every time had been different, every time better, in some undefined way.

No wonder she hadn't been able to focus on her work. She was still trying to count up the different ways he'd made love to her, the number of orgasms he'd brought her to in just one night.

'Hmm?' she murmured vaguely; some hint of a message had been in Millie's words that was struggling to strike a chord.

'I could never do these fancy mudcake or cream-puff things,' Millie continued, pointing to a picture of a *croquembouche*. 'Mine were more the old-fashioned type. But these are pretty.'

Finally her words worked their way through the fog that had been Sophie's morning. She swung her chair around. 'You make wedding cakes?'

Millie looked abashed. 'Well, I used to. I once won a bake-off competition with my fruit-cake recipe. I'm not so good at learning fancy new stuff—like all this Vietnamese and Thai cuisine I know Mr Caruana would like, for instance—but I do a pretty mean classic wedding cake.'

Sophie couldn't believe what she was hearing. 'Monica wants a traditional cake. Something like—' She scrabbled through the papers on her desk for a copy of the old photograph, diving on it when she found it. 'Something like this.'

'Oh!' Millie took the copy and gave a wistful sigh. 'So that's her parents, then. I never met them, you know. But doesn't Monica resemble her mother so?'

Sophie agreed. The likeness was uncanny, whereas Daniel seemed more of a blend, the strength of his father's nose and jawline coupled with the high cheek-bones and generosity of his mother's lips.

'Oh, and that cake,' Millie continued. 'I made one just like it for Sybil Martin's wedding, only we had fresh roses rather than orchids.' She shook her head and clucked. 'Hard work, keeping those roses fresh-looking in this climate, I tell you. We had them in the cooler until the last moment.'

'You made a cake like this?'

'A piece of cake!' the older woman said before laughing at her own joke.

'Millie, do you think you could you make one for Monica and Jake? In return, maybe I could teach you how to cook Thai. It's dead easy, really. Much easier than producing a wedding cake.'

The woman's smile vanished, though there was just the tiniest glimmer of interest mixed with the disbelief in her eyes. 'You really want me to have a go at a wedding cake, then?'

'I'm serious. I'd pay you, of course. I wouldn't expect you to do all that work for nothing. And we'll have a Thai cooking-class first chance we get.'

Daniel let himself into the house, weary, hot and disgruntled. His day had been a waste. The fallout from the aborted Townsville conference had consumed most of the day's overt efforts, while secretly he'd been waiting for his phone to beep, waiting for the message that would spell the end to his affair with Sophie. Because there was no way Fletcher would turn down two million in cold, hard cash, surely?

Something good wafted from the direction of the kitchen, spicy, aromatic and flavoured with garlic, ginger and fresh herbs; his stomach growled so appreciatively he had to investigate for himself, if only to grab a beer and find out how long it would be before he could eat.

The last thing he expected to find was both his women in the kitchen, Millie and Sophie wearing matching pinnies and engrossed in cooking up a storm. Millie noticed him first.

'Mr Caruana, I didn't hear you come in.'

He wasn't surprised, there were so many pans and woks simmering on the hotplates the extractor could hardly keep up. But it was Sophie's reaction he was more taken by. She looked up from whatever she was chopping, her eyes shadowed by her long lashes, and he could swear she was doing that blushing thing again.

Millie pressed a cold beer into his hands. 'Sophie's giving me a lesson on how to cook Thai. I hope you're hungry. We've got a veritable feast in store for you.'

He levered the cap off his beer and pulled out one of the bar stools along the wide kitchen bench, uncharacteristically plonking himself down; usually he'd head straight to his office. 'You didn't tell me you could cook, Sophie.'

She looked sideways at him, the knife in her hands suddenly stilled. 'I can do lots of things.'

Oh, now that he *did* know. Already he was looking forward to finding out more. He raised the open bottle to her. 'Here's to discovering your other hidden talents.' And he smiled when her blush deepened. How could she be so shy on the one hand, when she was so explosive in bed? But then he remembered the woman last night standing half-hidden by the doors, as if embarrassed by her nakedness, and he wondered again at how inexperienced she seemed. She hadn't been a virgin, but she couldn't have had too many men, that was for certain. One of them would surely have whisked her off the market by now.

He was pondering the significance of that thought when the phone in his pocket beeped, souring both the taste of his beer and his lighter mood-change since walking in the door.

Sophie, on the other hand, seemed suddenly brighter. 'Oh, but you'll never guess what—Millie used to make wedding cakes. She's agreed to make Monica and Jake's. Isn't that great?'

Suddenly his beer wasn't just sour; now it tasted like crap.

He pushed himself from the chair, leaving the half-empty bottle on the bench. 'I have a call to make.'

'Don't take too long,' Millie called behind him. 'Dinner will be ready in twenty minutes.'

He slammed his office door with unnecessary force, making the windows rattle. How could Sophie do that? How could she pretend the wedding was going ahead when she knew damned well it wasn't? He paced the wall of his office, end to end and back again, finding no answers, no reason.

And how could she drag Millie into it, getting her hopes up about making some bloody wedding cake for a wedding that was destined to be a non-event from the start?

Why did she persist with this whole wedding-planner fantasy, anyway? Was she so desperate to convince him that it was real that she needed to involve his personal staff? Did she really believe Millie's involvement would sway him? Now she was only going to let Millie down when it all came unstuck.

None of it made sense, least of all whatever it was gnawing at the recesses of his mind. She was a good actress. She had to be, to pretend the wedding was real and to suck everyone into her plan.

Yet what kind of actress could blush on demand? What kind of actress could turn shyness into an art?

Was Jo wrong about her motives? Did Sophie actually believe the wedding was real? Nothing he'd witnessed so far gave any hint that her efforts to get this wedding underway were half-hearted.

And nothing she'd done gave any hint that she'd got wind of his million-dollar offer to her brother. Sure, it would pay her to keep quiet until the deal was done if she was getting the cut Jo suggested, but wouldn't he have noticed just a glimmer of interest once the game was on?

Was she cleverer than that, too clever and too interested in a hefty-dollar payout to give herself away?

Or was her brother playing her for a fool, using her as his blind while he sucked the bride's brother dry?

The idea appealed, made a sick kind of sense. Fletcher had no loyalty to his sister; they'd only known each other a few short years, after all. She and her wedding-planner business was just a cover, her business's need for capital a mere coincidence. He refused to believe she was part of Fletcher's plan.

He sat down on the edge of his desk, the pieces reassembling themselves in his mind. Sophie's brother was playing her for a fool. She and her wedding-planning business validated his story, that was all.

And, once Fletcher had the money, he'd run, leaving both Monica and Sophie high and dry, and leaving Daniel to pick up the pieces.

Someone like Fletcher would do that.

The phone in his pocket beeped again, reminding him he had messages waiting—reminding him that whatever he thought or hoped probably wasn't the issue. He had to deal in facts.

So he checked his messages, found the one from Jo he'd been expecting and opened it: *Fletcher and Co on three day cruise. Offer made. Awaiting response on return.*

He snorted, letting go some of the angst he'd felt building from the first time his phone had beeped. So Fletcher was making the most of Hawaii's attractions while he was there, and no doubt Monica too. He knew he should feel angrier. He knew his gut should be rebelling at the prospect of his sister with that man.

Only it didn't, and it wasn't, and it was all because of one thing: *he had Fletcher's sister.*

No news was definitely good news. Three days would be more than enough. Fletcher would have to accept defeat this time and more than likely Daniel would have had his fill of Sophie. They all paled after a while, no matter how tempting they'd been in the beginning. Sophie was good, he granted her that, but three days surely had to be enough for this crazy fire to burn out?

More than enough.

There was a tap at the door and it slowly opened. 'Daniel?' the subject of his thoughts said tentatively. 'Dinner's ready if you are.'

He was at her side in a heartbeat, determined to make the most of the next three days. He curled his hand around her neck and hauled her into his kiss. 'Oh,' he said after she'd been thoroughly and deeply kissed so that her taste and scent filled his senses, stoking the flames of that fire once more. 'Believe me, I'm ready.'

They made love in the plunge-pool afterwards, a slow, delicious tangling of bodies, tongues and limbs, an exquisite pleasure-filled torture where delay heightened desire and where postponing the inevitable increased the need. Until finally, their eyes driven dark with desperation, they came together in a writhing, heaving conflagration that churned the water until it was white with foam.

Later, when both the water and their heartbeats had calmed and she lay like a sleepy cat against his body, he wondered about those three days being enough. He'd just had the best sex of his life; the way this woman felt under his hand, the way his body reacted to that touch, there was plenty more to come.

She stirred in his arms and stretched deliciously against him, her eyes fluttering to wakefulness—but it was the smile she gave him, a heady mix of innocence and temptation that made him feel that the bottom had just dropped out of the pool. 'Thank you,' she said, her hand lazily stroking his chest.

He picked it up, took it to his mouth and kissed it before softly dropping it down again. 'For what?'

'Lots of things. For sex in the pool. And sex on the deck. And sex in the shower. I don't think I'll forget that for a while.'

He found himself grinning along with her. Was it only last night they'd first come together? They'd made love so many times already, it felt like it must be longer.

'My pleasure,' he growled, meaning it, liking the way her fingers had found his nipple, how her nails raked tiny circles around its peak.

'I never knew it could be so good—the sex, I mean. Not that I've had that much experience, of course. Not like you, I imagine. You've probably had loads and loads of women.'

That many? He couldn't recall. 'Does it matter? You're the best so far.' She blushed, the way she did, but this time she seemed to blush all over.

'Yeah, sure.'

He didn't know why he'd admitted it, but it was out there now, and he wasn't about to argue the point. 'So, how many lovers have you had?'

She screwed up her nose. 'It's a bit embarrassing really. Only the one. Two, really, if you count the first time, but really just one.'

'So who was he?'

'A guy I met. I did a volunteer programme for a year doing English as a second language in a small village in Thailand.'

'That's where you learned to cook so well?'

'You really liked it?' Her head lifted from his shoulder, her eyes bright with pleasure.

'I loved it,' he said, kissing her on the tip of her nose. 'Thank you.'

She snuggled her head back down, the water lapping at their joined skin. 'I'm glad. Anyway, Craig was another volunteer from New Zealand. We were the only foreigners, and it was pretty isolated. I was homesick, and Mum had just got sick—not too bad, at that stage, but I was worried about her because I had six months left on my contract, and…'

'And Craig was there.'

Her fingers made whirls in his chest hair. 'And Craig was there. He was a nice enough guy, but we knew it was temporary. Kind of like sticking on a plaster: it helped cover the wound when I was a bit sad and lonely.'

He nodded. 'So who was the other one?'

She screwed up her nose again.

'That was a bit more embarrassing. I had a bit of a crush on this guy at school. Anyway, someone laced the punch with alco-pop at the end-of-school party and Simon and I got a bit carried away—maybe more than a bit, if you know what I mean. It was awful. We were both so horrified, we never spoke to each other again.'

He knew what she meant. He'd done his own fair share of experimenting when he was in high school. *Until he and Emma had become an item.*

God, he didn't want to think about Emma now. Not here, not while he was screwing Fletcher's sister.

He pushed away, letting go of her as he sat up, his head in his hands, waiting for the explosion of pain he knew would come. The guilt at his betrayal that he should be sleeping with this woman.

That he would be *enjoying* it, after what Fletcher had done!

And the pain came, though nowhere near as intense as he had expected. Dulled through too much sex, he assumed. It was a wonder he had feelings left at all.

'What's wrong?'

He looked skyward, to the blanket of stars and moon overhead, and sighed. 'It's late and I've got an early start. Let's go to bed.'

Whatever had been bothering him that night—first in disappearing so abruptly into his office before dinner, and then his all-too-rapid change of mood in the pool—it hadn't hung around. Sophie looked dreamily out of the window of her office, wondering if she'd ever regain the ability to focus for longer than two minutes at a time. The last few days and nights had been amazing and it was hard to imagine a time when sex or memories of their love-making hadn't figured so prominently in her life.

But how could she—as someone who had never hungered for the touch of a man, who had never missed it from her neatly ordered life—suddenly be so obsessed by the sensations stirred within her?

And how could Daniel make her feel the way he did with just one look, one caress? How could he reduce her to nothing more than a mass of screaming nerve endings again and again?

Those nerve endings made themselves known to her now. She looked at the clock; he would be home soon. He'd been coming home earlier and earlier every day. When Millie had commented on it, he'd said there wasn't much on, but he'd winked at her while he said it and had given her *that* look and whisked her off to the bedroom before dinner. And last night he'd had Millie prepare a picnic basket and they'd had dinner on the private beach in the cove below, taking turns at swimming, making love and feeding each other with treats from the basket.

If he kept this up, a girl could almost think she was special. *Almost.*

If he hadn't told her that she was his best lover so far, she might already believe she was. For, even if he'd been telling her the truth that night, his words had been a stark reminder that she was one of many and that Daniel was used to moving on.

As he would no doubt do again.

With a sigh she forced her thoughts back to the reason why she was here—to organise a wedding, not fall head over heels with Daniel Caruana. There was no future in it, no point to their relationship. Because even if their affair lasted that long once Monica and Daniel were married there was no reason for her to stay on the island, no reason not to return to Brisbane.

She refused to look at the clock again, to see how much or how little the minute hand had moved since she'd last looked. She had to keep her head, not lose her heart.

If only he didn't make it so difficult.

The computer on the desk behind pinged with incoming mail: hopefully confirmation at the last of the printing job's completion. She turned to her desk, happy to have an excuse to think about work, and clicked on her email programme. She smiled when she saw it was from Jake instead. She opened it, thinking they must be back from their cruise, wondering how it had gone even as her smile turned to a frown.

I need to talk to you. Urgently. Are you alone?
J

She stared vacantly at the message, hit reply with trembling fingers and sent off a brief message.

Bare seconds later, her phone buzzed. 'Jake,' she said, 'what's wrong? Is Monica okay?'

'She's fine. She's at the hairdresser. We're both fine.' But he sounded anything but, his words tight and clipped and angry as hell. 'I need to give you a message for Caruana.'

'Sure, what is it?'

'Tell him I don't want his money. Tell him to call off his dogs.'

Her blood ran cold. 'What money?' But somehow she knew before he'd uttered another word.

'The money he offered me to dump Monica. We hadn't been here ten minutes and his thug was on the phone, offering me half a million to leave her cold.'

'He offered you that?' Sophie dropped into her chair. It was an obscene amount of money, but what she'd been doing with Daniel while he'd been plotting to rid himself of her brother and this marriage was more obscene.

She'd slept with him, practically offered herself to him.

And, all the while he'd been pretending to go along with the plans she'd been making, he was busy planning to ensure the wedding never happened.

'That was just the opening gambit,' her brother continued. 'I told him to get lost and he's upped the offer to a cool million now.'

Something squeezed tight in her chest. This couldn't be happening. Why would Daniel want her here, organising a wedding he was busy trying to ensure would never happen? She'd actually believed he was coming round to the idea.

Yet hadn't Daniel practically boasted how he'd got rid of Monica's previous boyfriends?

Despite everything, despite all she knew and suspected, she still had to ask the question. 'You're sure it's Daniel?'

'Oh, yeah. It's him. And this thug who calls himself security—Jo Dimitriou—I know him, but I didn't know he was working for Caruana now. I've got this really bad feeling about him. Watch out for him. He's dangerous.'

And Daniel wasn't? Jo gave her the creeps, she was the first to agree, but who was the more dangerous—the man who offered you money at someone else's behest, or the man who made you believe in one thing when he was busy destroying everything you were trying to build up while you were looking the other way? 'I should have warned you, Jake. He's done this before—offered money, I mean—to get rid of Monica's boyfriends.'

'Bastard! Monica told me she was beginning to think if there was something wrong with her, not being able to hold onto a man.'

'What are you going to do?'

'Stay here for now. I figure Monica's better off out of it. I haven't told her yet. She thinks the sun shines out of her darling brother.'

'I understand.'

'Listen, Sophie, I've told this Jo guy no. There's clearly no way Caruana's going to listen to me, but if he hears it from you he might actually believe it. Can you tell him? Tell him to save his efforts? It doesn't matter what he offers me, the answer's still no. Tell him I'm marrying his sister, whether he likes it or not.'

Sophie put the phone down, her mind numb, her body in shock, and a great, gaping hole where her heart should have been. She'd thought she'd been wrong about him. She'd thought it had been the shock of the wedding announcement that had turned him into a raging monster that first day, and that he was coming round—*had* come round—to accepting that the wedding would go ahead. Bit by bit, he'd seemed to soften.

Or was that her? Falling into his bed and wanting to believe he was different, so that her first impressions had been wrong. Seduced by sex until she'd believed the monster was the lie, that the man was better than that.

When clearly he'd been a monster all along.

She looked around the office: at the pictures she'd stuck up on the walls; at the various lists that seemed to cover every horizontal surface; at the samples of stationery and swatches of fabrics she had for colour matching.

Daniel had no intention of this wedding going ahead. So what was she even doing here?

From down the hallway came the sound of voices and she had to fight the sudden urge to retch.

Daniel was home.

It had been the day from hell. A bank in one of his shopping centres had been host to a hold up, there'd been another blow-up with the Townsville negotiations, which meant he'd have to head back up there first thing tomorrow, and Jo had been giving him grief about upping Fletcher's offer again in the wake of this latest rejection. And the worst thing about that was the random thought he'd had that maybe Fletcher's reluctance to accept an offer meant Fletcher really did love his sister. He'd shoved the idea away as quickly as it had arisen, but the sick feeling had lingered all afternoon.

If he hadn't had Sophie to come home to, there would have been nothing to make the day worth living.

Millie handed him a beer and he chugged half of it down before drawing breath. 'Thanks, I needed that,' he said, looking around, surprised Sophie wasn't hanging around the kitchen where he usually found her this time of day. 'Where is she?' he asked.

'Still working in that office of hers, I imagine. Probably didn't hear you come in. Why don't you go and pry her away from that computer? She's been in there all day.'

It would be his pleasure. The second half of the beer met the same fate as the first, and he put the empty bottle down. He was feeling better already.

He'd already kicked off his shoes and unbuttoned his shirt by the time he was halfway to her office. If he had to pry her away from her computer, he didn't want to waste any time on the basics.

Already he could feel her cool hands on his skin, feel the flick of her tongue over his straining tip, feel her trembling with need beneath him in that hitched moment of anticipation before he lunged into her.

Oh yeah; already he was feeling a *lot* better.

The door was open and he found her standing by the windows, her back to the door. Just one glance and already he'd worked out how he was going to get her out of the little strappy number she wore in the minimum time. 'Knock knock,' he said.

Then she turned, and a foul day turned belly up.

She looked like the eye of a storm, he thought, the brief moment of respite after one onslaught and before all hell broke loose. She stood as straight as a pillar, her features drawn tight, her eyes ice-cold and malevolent, the storm building within; he wondered what the hell had happened to bring this on. Just this morning she'd been telling him she couldn't wait for him to come home. And now this?

Maybe he'd been right. Maybe three days had been long enough for whatever it was to burn out. A pity, in that case, given Fletcher had said no to this latest offer, that potentially they had more time together before it must inevitably end.

But the thought that she might have lost interest first irked him. He'd assumed he'd be the one to know when it was over.

'How was your day?' he asked, determined not to be swept into her foul mood. If she wanted to tell him whatever was bugging her, that was fine, but he was no masochist. He wasn't about to go poking about, looking. Better to turn to something he knew she could talk about ad infinitum. 'Get lots of wedding things organised?'

Her head jerked up, her eyes flashing fire. 'And you really care because…?'

He'd provoked a response, that was something, not that she'd given him any clues with it. 'I'll admit, talking weddings doesn't hold the same appeal for me as it does for you. But don't let that stop you. There's nothing I adore more at the end of a long day than being regaled with tales of the latest decision about flowers or decorations or the advantages of two tiers versus three.'

'You bastard!'

The words didn't stick. He'd been called much worse in his time, no doubt would be again. But it didn't help that he hadn't spoken the complete truth. He had no interest in her pointless wedding arrangements, that was true, but at the end of his work day he'd liked nothing more than hearing her talk. He didn't care about what, he'd just loved her enthusiasm and energy and hearing the laughter in her voice.

But there was no laughter now.

'I don't know what's bothering you, but clearly you're in no mood for company. If you'll excuse me?'

He'd barely made it to the door when he heard the words. 'Did you offer Jake money to break off with Monica?'

So she wasn't in on it. That was his first thought. He'd suspected Fletcher was taking advantage of her all along and he was right. *So why would he have told her now?*

But that didn't matter. What mattered right now was that she knew and that was why she was so angry. *Damn.* He spun around. 'Did he tell you that?'

'Answer the question! Did you, or that henchman you call a security boss, offer Jake money to break off with Monica? Seems to me it's got your *modus operandi* written all over it.'

He stiffened and dragged in a breath. So the truth was out. There was no point denying it, even if he wished she didn't know. Even if he wished for that other Sophie back, the warm, sensual woman who responded to his touch as if she was made for it. But that Sophie was gone, probably for ever, and even though part of him ached inexplicably at the thought he'd always known it would happen some time.

And now he could only defend his actions. His record might damn him in her eyes, but history was on his side, after all. 'He'll say yes. They all do.'

He watched her almost crumple in a heap. Her fisted hands came up over her face as her knees buckled beneath her. But she didn't fall. She pushed herself up straight, thrust her arms away and glared at him, her eyes like polished stone. 'For God's sake, Daniel. Can't you see? Jake *loves* Monica.'

'So he *says*.'

'Because it's the truth! And he asked me to tell you he doesn't want your money, whether it's five-hundred thousand, or a million, or whatever else you decide to throw at him. He doesn't want it because he's marrying Monica, whatever you want to believe in your tortured, twisted mind.'

He frowned. She had the numbers wrong, but then she was hysterical and there was no point correcting her.

'I thought you'd changed,' she continued, her voice softer, resigned, with a hint of melancholy. 'I thought the fact you insisted the wedding would be held here, the way you insisted I should stay to make all the arrangements on site…' She shook her head, her eyes uncomfortably direct as they searched his out. 'I know you're desperate to protect your sister because she's all you have, and you've been looking after her ever since your parents died, but I thought for once that you might be more interested in her happiness than shutting her off from the world. I thought that over the last few days you were at least coming to terms with this wedding, even if you couldn't openly embrace it.'

She drew breath, kicked up her chin. 'I thought there might actually be hope for you. I'm sorry. I was wrong.'

Her last few words were the kick that set his blood pressure rocketing. She didn't know him. She didn't know the first thing about him. And yet she stood there and made out that he was some kind of disappointment?

'You don't know the first thing about it!'

'I know you can't bear the thought of anyone else loving your sister, so much so that you pay anyone who gets close to get rid of them.'

His spun round, needing to hit something, his open palm slamming against the wall before he turned back. 'And you don't think I have reason?'

'Sure you have reason—you're jealous they'll steal her away from you—and you use the excuse of them being nothing more than fortune-hunters to drive them away.'

'No!' With a few purposeful strides he was before her. 'Did Monica tell you about her first boyfriend, the charming Cal, her first *true love*?'

Sophie backed away, her eyes wide, but there was strength in them too, he could see, and a determination not to be cowed. In the very next moment her chin cocked up. 'Not specifically. She said she'd had a few boyfriends but none of them had stuck around long. And we all know why that is, don't we?'

'Do we? Let me tell you about Cal. He was ambitious and determined to make a million dollars before he was twenty-one.'

'And this was a reason to resent him? Didn't you do something similar yourself?'

'Not that way. Not by blackmailing the brother of the girl you're supposed to be in love with. Not with a movie of them having sex.'

Her eyes widened and he awarded himself a mental victory. At last she might begin to understand where he was coming from. 'He did what?'

'Either I paid up or he'd plaster the images all over the Internet. My sister. Her first time. Do you know what that does to a brother when you're supposed to be looking out for her? Of course I paid him out.'

'Daniel, I had no idea.'

'No, you didn't. You were too happy to judge from a distance. But maybe now you can understand why I never hesitated to get in first with an offer, before any damage was done, before they found a way to extract it by other means. And they took it. Which proves something, wouldn't you say?'

'It proves that this Cal was a monster. It proves that maybe they weren't deeply involved with Monica and taking the money was easier. But it doesn't mean that every man is like that. And it doesn't mean that Monica should be punished for ever. Don't you think she deserves a chance at happiness?

Or do you intend dispensing with every man she ever shows an interest in, ensuring she leads a long, lonely life thinking there is something wrong with her. Is that what you want?'

He looked skywards. Of course he didn't want that. He wanted his sister happy, with a man who would put her on the pedestal she deserved, not some fortune-hunter. 'She'll find someone worthy of her one day.'

'What about Jake? Doesn't it occur to you that the reason he's saying no to your offers is because it's not the money he wants? He loves Monica. Can't you see that?'

'He's not marrying my sister!'

'What is your problem? What have you got against my brother, other than the fact he grew up poor and you grew up rich. Maybe he gave you some schoolboy grief at high school? What else did he ever do to you?'

'What did he do to me?' He laughed as blood fired the furnace of his eyes, painting her outline red. 'Your sweet and innocent Jake did nothing, nothing at all, apparently. Clearly I should welcome him into the bosom of my family.'

The tone of his voice put chills down her spine. 'Tell me,' she said, simultaneously too afraid to hear, too frightened not to find out what it was that had driven this man to such bitterness and to take the measures he had. 'Why is it that you hate Jake so much?'

'Why wouldn't I hate him?' He looked at her then, his eyes suddenly empty shells, lost, lonely and soulless. 'Because your brother killed my fiancée.'

CHAPTER ELEVEN

His fiancée? *Oh God*. She remembered the photo in the guest room, the smiling girl Millie had said had died in tragic circumstances, and whose picture Daniel couldn't bear either to part with or to see. But what could her brother possibly have had to do with her death?

Nothing.

'No.' Sophie wasn't even sure why she'd believed that, but she did and it was out there; now the word hung between them, a one-word rebuttal to an accusation of nightmarish proportions. 'You're wrong.'

'You don't even know him. You don't know what he was like back then. You have no idea what he was capable of!'

'Maybe not, but I still don't believe my brother is the type of man that could have done what you said and be lining up to marry your sister. What kind of man could do such a thing? I'm telling you now, Jake's not that man.'

'Then you don't know your brother at all.'

She shook her head. 'No. I don't know you.' She moved to go past and he caught her arm, his fingers like claws in her flesh, although she felt no pain, her fury consuming her ability to feel anything else.

'Don't you want to hear what he did? Or are you too scared to learn the truth about your precious brother?'

He was wound tight as a drum, his skin like a mask over the bones of his face, his eyes deep pits as he challenged her, continuing unbidden, his voice empty and flat. 'It was our final year at high school. We'd just finished exams and my family all went to Italy for three months, to visit the extended family my parents hadn't seen for years. Emma and I were to be officially engaged the week after we came back.'

He seemed to realise he was still holding her then, and let her go, turning his head away. 'Emma wanted to come with us, but she'd just scored a job and we thought it was better to start saving up. Three months away from her seemed an eternity—stupid, really, when I had no idea then what eternity even meant.'

He paused, his head dipped on sagging shoulders. 'I couldn't wait to get on that plane home. Except just before we left for the airport we got a phone call. Emma had been thrown from a car when it careened off the road. She wasn't wearing a seat belt. Maybe she might have survived the crash if she was, maybe she might have survived anyway, but the car rolled on top of her. She didn't have a chance.'

Sophie shivered, the chill of his words going bone-deep. He'd lost his fiancée in tragic circumstances, then he'd lost his parents in a similar way not long after. No wonder the trauma had cut so deep.

'I'm truly sorry,' she said, meaning it. 'But I still don't understand what that had to do with my brother.'

His eyes turned to black holes. 'She was in your brother's car!'

Sophie swallowed. She knew Jake sometimes had head-aches, a legacy of a crash he'd once been in, but she'd had no idea of the details. Was Daniel right? Did she really not know her brother that well? Could he be responsible for such a tragedy?

'And you blame him?'

'Who else am I supposed to blame? He always resented that I had money and he had none. He was jealous of my success at sport and my academic results. And he hated the fact the most beautiful girl at school wasn't interested in him, despite his efforts. So, the moment my back was turned and I was away, he went after her.'

'You can't know that, surely? Just because they happened to be in the same car together.'

'Oh, I know it.' His lips turned into a thin line. 'Because there's more—the autopsy discovered she was pregnant.' He tilted his head and directed eyes of bleak, black ice at her. 'The baby wasn't mine.'

'You're sure?'

'How could it be, when we'd never had sex? We were waiting for the engagement, which was half the reason I couldn't wait to get back.'

'And you think it was Jake's child?'

'She was six weeks' pregnant. I'd been gone three months. She was with him when she died. You work it out.'

She swallowed. The horror of the past was so vast, ugly and heinous right here in this room, wound tight inside this man, that she wanted to flee from it and from the island for ever. Because now that horror belonged to her too, courtesy of her brother's involvement, courtesy of Daniel's callous seduction of her. And still she couldn't believe it could be true; she wished she could find the words to console Daniel for his loss, wished she could find the words to defend her brother before she could talk to him and determine the truth herself.

But another thought intruded, another gut-churning question demanding to be answered: 'Why am I here, then, organising a wedding that you never had any intention of holding? Were you just trying to pretend to Monica that you actually cared about her happiness? Or did you somehow think, in your twisted mind, that sleeping with me was how you intended getting even with my brother?'

He flinched and growled out his response. 'Does it actually matter?'

She decided it didn't. But she'd be damned if she'd give him the satisfaction of running away. 'I hate you for what you've done to your sister. I hate you for the way you've treated Jake. Most of all I hate you for what you've done to me.

'But, mark my words, this wedding is going to happen,' she said with a resolve tapped from a well she didn't know she possessed. 'Something awful happened all those years ago, yes, but I don't believe that Jake could have done what you say he did—and I'm going to prove it. And then that wedding is going to go ahead right here, right under your nose. And you're going to suck it up!'

She wasn't leaving. Somehow as Daniel stared blindly out at the pristine view of sea and sky, that one piece of information filtered through the morass of his mind and settled like a feather in the foreground. In a day when everything that could possibly have gone wrong had gone wrong, at least he'd salvaged that.

She wasn't leaving.

He wasn't even sure why it was so important. She'd been going to leave some time anyway; it had been inevitable from day one. But it was strange how the concept of her departure had gone from something he'd treated as a cold inevitability to something he'd been happy to avoid every time Fletcher had turned down the latest offer. Because the sex was so good?

Must be.

Although it might take some doing, getting her back in his bed after today. Damn. What a waste.

He turned and sighed. Did she really believe this wedding could go ahead after what he'd told her about her brother? She was either blindly loyal or blindly stupid, yet in a way he could almost admire her devotion to her brother. Wasn't it how he felt about Monica? He'd do anything for her.

Except stand by when she married Jake Fletcher.

The call came when he was back in his room, and because it came from Jo he picked up. If something was happening in Hawaii, he needed to know. 'What's up?'

'I doubled the offer. Thought you should know.'

'What the hell for? I told you to wait.'

'Because you've got to get rid of him! He's scum, Dan, you know that. You don't want him marrying your sister. Isn't it bad enough that right this minute he's probably screwing her?'

'Shut up, Jo!' He didn't need to hear the words. He didn't need those pictures in his head.

'She'll be banged up, just like that other one, if you don't get rid of him. I'm just trying to do my job.'

Are you? Daniel wondered, one hand massaging his pounding temple. If he didn't know better, he'd think Jo was more interested in railroading this wedding than he was, when it was he who had the issue with Fletcher.

Then again, it was probably just Jo's overactive loyalty kicking in again. After all, he'd seen the damage Fletcher had inflicted upon him before. No doubt he didn't want to have to scrape him off the floor again.

'Okay, Jo. The four million is offered now. Let it go at that. But don't make any more offers without my okay. Got that?'

'What happened?' Sophie cried when her brother picked up the phone, 'He thinks you killed his fiancée; he thinks you got her pregnant. What happened that day?'

'Sophie, hold on. I have to change phones.' She heard the rush of movement, the echo of a second connection before the first clicked off, and the sound of a door being shut before her brother picked up again, his voice low. 'Sophie's dozing. I don't want her to hear.'

'Maybe you should tell her. Maybe you should tell all of us. I told Daniel I didn't believe him, but it's too awful. I can't fight this battle for you, Jake. I thought I could smooth the waters between you, but he hates you, and the way he tells it I can't see a way through. Please tell me it's all a lie.'

'Sophie, I'm sorry. I should have told you. Believe me, I wanted to, but how can I when I don't know the whole picture myself?'

'What do you mean?'

'I should have said something, but it's hard for me. Even now…' Down the line she heard the rasp of his breath, as though it physically pained him to have to remember. 'I survived the accident but I was in a coma for two months. I still get flashbacks and nightmares, but I still can't remember clearly what happened just before the crash.'

'You can't? But you have to, Jake. It's the only way.'

'Listen, Sophie, the doctors think my memories of those minutes may never be recovered. All I have is fragments and impressions, but they may mean nothing, the doctors think, or they may be scenarios I've come up with since to explain in my mind what happened.'

She swallowed and wiped away moisture she hadn't realised she'd shed from her cheek. 'What do you think happened?'

There was a long sigh at the end of the line and a sound like he had slid down the wall to the floor. 'I have this impression—this feeling—that Emma came to me for help that night. We weren't really good friends but we'd talked sometimes at school—when Caruana wasn't around, that was. I'd heard they were getting married and I didn't see her all summer. Until that night.'

Sophie heard his ragged breaths as he paused, willing him silently to continue so that she could make sense of the horror of that night, make sense of everything that had happened since.

'It was raining heavily, and I have this impression of her standing on the doorstep, soaked through, her eyes swollen with tears. I can't remember the words, but it was all mixed up with the baby and Jo and Daniel coming home. She was scared, desperate to get away. *But I can't remember why!*'

'It's okay, Jake,' she said, wishing he wasn't locked alone in a bathroom half a world away, wishing she could be there to hold him. 'Take your time.'

'I'm okay.' He sighed. 'And then I have this picture, like a photo in my mind, of Emma behind the steering wheel, with me beside her yelling at her to stop. But she didn't stop. We were both thrown from the car. The police didn't believe I wasn't driving.'

'And the baby? Was it yours?'

'I swear to God I never slept with her, Sophie. I didn't see her all summer before that night.'

She let go a breath that carried much more than just air. 'But everyone assumed you were.'

'I didn't wake up for two months, and by that time everyone believed it. Emma was dead and buried and people were starting to come to terms with it. What point would there have been in digging it all up again?'

'So you let them go on thinking it?'

'It never mattered, Sophie, because I could live with myself. I knew I hadn't done the wrong thing and that was good enough. But it mattered when I fell in love with Monica and found out who her brother was. I tried to talk to him; I knew we had to sort it out some time. But he wouldn't return my calls. And what could I really tell him that he'd believe anyway?'

'I understand.'

He sighed. 'I'm sorry. I know it was asking too much of you, but I was really hoping that if I disappeared with Monica he might get used to the idea. I thought he'd have to. I see now I was running away when I should have stayed and dealt with it myself. I'm sorry to drop you in it like that, Soph. It must have been a nightmare for you, putting up with him all this time.'

'It had its moments,' she said quietly. 'But I'm glad you told me at last. You know you have to tell Daniel. He has to know the truth.'

'Even though I don't know it all? Why would he ever believe it wasn't my baby?'

'You have to try.'

'Yeah, I guess you're right. Maybe we'll come back early. At least then it might put an end to these offers I've been getting.'

Sophie's ears pricked up. 'You've had more?'

'It's up to one and half million. Nice work, if you can get it.'

Fury welled up inside her. What would it take to make Daniel believe it? 'I told him, Jake. I told him you weren't interested.'

'It's okay. It means I need to come back, in that case, so I can tell him where to shove his money myself. There's no way we're going to sort this out with text messages.'

She heard the muffled sound of a woman's voice and a knocking. 'Soph, I've got to go. Talk to you tomorrow.'

'I'm moving to one of the cabins,' she said matter-of-factly over an untouched plate of mushroom risotto. She'd only come to the dinner table to tell him what she was intending to do, not to eat. 'I'll continue my work from there, which makes sense, given we'll be having the reception at the long-house pavilion.'

Across the table from her, he put down his fork. 'You're still persisting with this farce of a wedding, then?'

'I spoke to Jake. He's coming back to talk to you. He's got things you need to know—need to hear. Like the fact Emma wasn't carrying his child.'

Daniel leaned back in his chair, arms sprawled lazily over the sides, but she knew there was nothing lazy about him, nothing relaxed. It hurt her to realise how much she missed those arms around her already. 'You need to talk to Jake about that. He can't remember the details, but—'

'How convenient.'

'Talk to him, Daniel, and hear it for yourself. You made your mind up all those years ago when my brother was lying in a coma and couldn't defend himself. Was that fair?'

'It was obvious!'

'Was it? Or was it easy when you needed someone to blame? Why not pick on the man who wasn't even conscious? That's what I call convenient.' She stood. 'Oh, and as for your latest offer, do I need to tell you where my brother suggested you shove your one and half million?'

He steepled his fingers. 'One and a half million?'

'That's the figure Jake quoted.'

He leaned forward, an uncomfortable sensation crawling its way down his back. 'Sophie, let me ask you a question. How is your business doing? I mean, cash wise. Everything all right?'

She shrugged, thrown off-balance, eyebrows pulled into a frown. 'Fine. We had such a great year last year, we're look-ing to either expand our operation, or invest in case things get tight.'

'I see.' Whatever had been crawling over his back found its way to his stomach and turned solid. He picked up his napkin from his lap and placed it on the table. Suddenly he wasn't hungry any more. 'And Sophie?'

'Yes?'

'I've got something to chase up now, and I have to be in Townsville tomorrow, but I'd like to talk to you when I get back. You meant that about staying in one of the cabins?'

She nodded uncertainly.

'Then I'll see you when I get back. All right?'

She nodded and he gave a thin smile, 'I'm glad you're not leaving.'

She walked blindly back to pack her things, feeling even more confused. The monster had retreated, a hint of the Daniel she loved back again.

She stopped dead.

Oh God.

Where the hell had that come from? No way could she love him. No way. Not after all the things he'd done and said, and after the way he'd done everything in his power to break up Jake and Monica. No way could anyone love a monster like that.

Even if she did love his body and loved the way he made her feel when he made love to her. *Had sex,* she corrected.

Although it had felt like more.

All her own misguided emotions, she knew. Because Daniel Caruana was still in love with a girl who'd died years ago. A girl he'd put up on some kind of pedestal of perfection. A girl he was still fighting for.

He wasn't capable of loving anyone else.

And yet, if she wasn't in love with him, why had she found it so impossible to leave? Why had she been so secretly thrilled when he'd told her he was glad she was staying? If she'd really been serious about leaving him, wouldn't she have moved back to Brisbane, or even to somewhere in Cairns where she'd be close enough to arrange things?

But no. She'd decided to stay on the island. Why?

Because she couldn't bear the thought of being too far away from him.

Even though he could never love her. Even though anything between then was doomed from the start on so many levels.

She'd known it was a kind of madness that first night they'd made love. She'd known it and still she'd persisted, refusing to pay heed to logic. And now she had the proof of her madness: she loved him. She blundered into the room she used as an office and dropped into a chair, her face in her hands.

What a mess.

Sophie didn't see him again that night and he was gone early in the morning, the sound of the chopper stirring her from a restless night's slumber in the guest room. The picture of Emma smiled out at her from the bureau and Sophie had found herself staring back at her long into the night.

How must it have felt to be loved by Daniel? And how special must Emma have been to earn that love? And why did she hurt so much because that would never be her?

With sleep-deprived eyes and a head thick with too many pointless ramblings, she packed up the last of her things onto a golf buggy and waved goodbye to Millie, who was waiting with a basket of lunch and other treats to stock her cabin. 'I'm so sorry things haven't worked out for you here, lovey. I've so enjoyed having another woman for company.'

'Me too,' she said, giving the older woman a squeeze. 'But I'll come and visit.'

Millie sniffed. 'Make sure you do.'

The cabin was dark and cool inside; whoever had prepared it for her arrival had thoughtfully turned on the air conditioner. Without turning on the light, she sank gratefully to the bed and closed her eyes.

What the hell was she supposed to do? Daniel was coming to talk tonight—about what? Hopefully tomorrow Jake and Monica might be back. She'd sent Jake an email so he'd know to call her on her mobile, although she hadn't bothered to fill him in on why. But she had to admit, it would be easier with Monica and Jake here if she wasn't living in Daniel's house and sleeping in his bed. Things were bound to be complicated and ugly enough without that, if they were to find a way through the next few weeks.

Was she even kidding herself to think there *was* a way through?

She forced herself from the bed. She had no choice but to think that way, which meant she better get herself up and organised.

The meeting had gone better than expected. The arguments the lawyers had voiced that had held things up the other day seemed to dissolve into nothingness, compared to the massive stumbling block they had been. Thank God. At least something was going right.

He loosened his tie, looking out of the windscreen for the familiar landmarks that would mean he was getting close. He wasn't going back to the office. They didn't expect him, and he had more important things on his mind—like working out how wrong he'd been.

Why had Jo betrayed him that way? He didn't know; it wasn't as if he didn't pay him enough as it was. But maybe he should have seen the writing on the wall when he'd insisted

Daniel pay more to get rid of Jake. The tone of his voice had had greed written all over it. Was that when he'd hatched his plan to steal half the funds for himself?

But it wasn't only the money. It was his lies that Sophie's business needed a cash injection, implying from the start she was involved with the scam. So Daniel had a reason to hate Fletcher. Why had *Jo* been so ready to crucify Sophie into the deal? What was in it for him?

Damn the man. And so much for his pleas to forgive him. Forgive him, nothing; loyalty only went so far. And Jo had shown him he had none at all.

He should have got rid of him years ago.

They rounded a point and the familiar shape of Kallista appeared before them, lush and beautiful, like the woman he couldn't wait to see. He wasn't entirely sure what he was going to say to her, but he was hoping that by the time he got there something would have occurred to him that would make sense to them both.

He was so glad she hadn't left. He'd spoken the truth when he'd said that. The idea of her leaving was anathema to him. And it wasn't because he wanted to get even with her brother—not any more.

Because Sophie belonged there. With him. He just had to make her see it.

After all that had happened, the call had still taken her by surprise. The tears that had followed were almost impossible to staunch, the knowledge that it had all been for nothing almost too much to bear. Sophie held the cool facecloth to her swollen eyes, glad at least she hadn't got far with her unpacking. It would save time.

She took a deep breath and pushed herself away from the bathroom cabinet on legs finally strong enough to support her, blinking away the last of the moisture that blurred her vision, trying to work out what to do next. A warm draught stirred her skirt and she looked around, surprised to find the screen door open. Strange; she was sure she'd shut it. But maybe someone had dropped by with the milk she'd requested and forgotten to shut it. Not that she'd need any supplies now.

She reached for the handle and caught a whiff of stale sweat and nicotine. Fear speared down her spine, clearing her vision quicker than anything, but not fast enough to dodge the hand that snaked out from behind the curtains and grabbed her wrist.

CHAPTER TWELVE

SHE screamed, sensing it was Jo before the glint of gold at his wrist and fingers confirmed it, even before a thick gravel voice told her to shut up. He shoved her back and let go and she stumbled against the coffee table, before collapsing against a bucket chair as the big man slid closed the doors and locked them, pulling the curtains shut so nobody could see inside. Fear seized her at the calm and purposeful way he went about his business, as if he had all the time in the world, almost as if it was a well-rehearsed drill. She shivered. Without taking her eyes from him, she pushed herself out of the chair, putting as many pieces of furniture between them as possible, 'What are you doing here?'

He sneered, his eyes bloodshot and evil as he turned. 'You little bitch. You cost me my job.'

'How?'

He moved towards her and she moved back slowly until she hit up against the kitchenette bench. 'What did you tell Daniel?'

'What are you talking about? I don't know. Nothing that concerns you.'

He moved closer, his eyes wild, and she edged sideways. The last thing she needed was to be stuck in a corner. 'You told him how much I offered your stupid brother.'

'I only told him what Jake told me! Why is that such a problem?'

'You think I was going to waste all Caruana's money on that scum?'

The penny dropped. 'You were planning on stealing it! You were going to take your cut, and you're mad at me because you got your filthy, fat fingers caught in the till. Don't try to pin it on me.'

He growled. 'I would have got away with it, too, if you hadn't shot your mouth off. You owe me!'

She rubbed the wrist that still stung from his grip, trying to work out distance and angles, knowing she had to keep him talking if she was to have any hope of getting out of here before…

Oh no. She wasn't going there.

He took a step closer and she knew she'd have to move soon. She wondered how long the bathroom door would last if she locked herself in, wondered if she'd be courting disaster to search for a decent knife in the kitchen drawer before she bolted. 'You should have got away, little lady, while you could. When Millie finally told me you were down here in the cabins, it was almost too good to be true. She didn't want to tell me, either. Dunno why.'

Fear snaked down her spine. 'What did you do to her?'

'She'll live,' he said with a leery grin as he rubbed his groin. 'And don't worry. I saved the best for you.'

She dragged in air, trying not to retch, looking for reason or an argument that might sway him. 'Daniel's going to be here any minute. We've got a meeting.'

He laughed. 'Nice try. He's in Townsville all day. Besides, he's obviously finished with you if you're down here by your-self. Did he decide he'd had enough and threw you out like yesterday's leftovers?'

Her hands guided her as she edged along the bench top, fingers chancing upon something cane—the basket Millie had given her. 'You don't know anything.'

'I know he only wanted you here because Fletcher was screwing his sister. An eye for an eye, a root for a root.'

His words hit some place she didn't want to go, and she shoved them aside before they could do any damage. 'You're disgusting!'

'And you're a slut, but I'm not choosy.' And then he smiled. 'Didn't he tell you he was the one who booked the Tropical Palms? Paid them a million in cold, hard cash to get you here?'

'You're lying.'

'Ask him yourself, at this *meeting*.' He laughed at his own joke and took another step closer but there was still a small dining setting between them and Sophie knew it was now or never. She grabbed the handle of the basket with one hand and flung her arm in an arc, letting the basket fly directly at him while she ran around the other way.

She saw a big, beefy arm go up to ward it off, and it bounced away, but not before raining down its contents on him. 'Bitch!'

But she was already at the door, her fingers working at the lock, sliding the glass doors open. He slammed into her from behind and she crashed against the glass with a scream, her fingers losing the handle, clutching at the curtains, pulling them from their tracks with a crash as he dragged her back. 'You'll pay for that!'

'Let me go!' She struggled against his more powerful frame, caught a handful of his face and raked her nails down, drawing blood. The back of his hand smashed across her cheek, cracking her head back and momentarily stunning her.

He bundled her in his arms and carried her to the bedroom, throwing her sprawling on the bed. She landed with a whump, rolling over, scooting up to the headboard as far as she could and folding herself into a ball, her hand rubbing her aching jaw. 'Jake said you were a bully.'

He snorted as he unhitched his belt, and she pulled her feet in tighter. 'Did he, now? What the hell would he know? He was unconscious for months. Nobody knows nothin'.'

Fear sliced through her like the blow from a scythe, fear and a strange kind of horrific understanding. 'What are you talking about?'

'Shut up.' He moved around the bed and she scooted to the other side.

'I'll scream.'

'Scream all you like, honey. Caruana's other bitch did too, and it only made it all the better for me. Almost as satisfying as when your brother got lumbered with the blame.'

Realisation hit her with lightning-bolt force. 'It was your baby! She went to my brother's that night because she was pregnant with your baby and she didn't know what to do.' And, like a second lightning-hit, a more sickening truth hit home. 'You raped her. The minute Daniel's back was turned, you raped her, and all the years you let my brother take the blame.'

'Do you ever shut up? C'mere bitch.' He leaned over and lunged with surprising speed for such a big man. She screamed as his big fist snared an ankle, screamed louder as he tugged her back down the bed until she was flat on her back.

'Let me show you what a real man can do.'

Panic made her lash out with her other foot. She felt a crack as she made contact with something that felt like a brick, a sudden rush of pain spearing up her leg so intense that she almost thought the yowl she heard had come from her, until blood spurted from his nose. 'Bitch!' he cried, before reaching for her again.

'Get off her, you bastard!'

And then the bed beside her seemed to explode with flailing limbs and flying fists and she rolled away, falling to the floor, wondering if she were caught in some cruel dream. Because Daniel wasn't due back for hours, yet somehow he was here.

Someone rushed to her aid, pulling her away from the mess of tangled, writhing bodies while others swarmed over the bed, finishing the job of subduing Jo that Daniel had started until he was led away, bleeding and unrepentant.

Daniel rushed to her side and held her close, making out that she was something precious. Like she meant something. She wanted to be grateful to him. She wanted to with all her heart.

Except it was too late.

Cairns Base Hospital was cool and clinical and with just the right amount of detachment Sophie needed. She breathed in the sterile atmosphere, steeling herself, knowing she'd need it for the next visitor. Especially when her heart felt like a bleeding mess.

If only her doctor had been by to discharge her already, she would have been gone before the nurse called to ask if she was up to having a visitor.

There was a knock at the door as she stuffed things into her bag and she turned to see him already filling the space. Damn. She turned away almost as quickly.

Damn. Damn. Damn. Why did he always have to look so good no matter what he was wearing? He looked like he'd just walked out of an article on 'Saturday-unshaven, designer-casual' from the pages of *GQ* magazine: the alpha-male edition.

'You're leaving?'

'The doctor's on his way. I'm expecting to be discharged. All observations in the range of normal, apparently. No residual trace of concussion.'

'I can take you home.'

She sighed, her hands stilling over the bag. Home. Now there was a concept. 'I've organised transport, thanks.'

'Sophie.' And when she turned back it was to find him right there, so close to her that she flinched. The terror of yesterday's events was much too recent, the fear that she might throw herself into his arms much too real. 'I'm sorry,' he said, dropping his lifted hand as he gave her space. 'But your cheek…'

'The swelling will fade, along with the bruises.' Besides, it was the bruises he couldn't see that hurt more. 'I guess it could have been worse.'

'I'm sorry.'

'What are you sorry for?' She managed a tremulous laugh as she shifted away. 'You're the one who saved me, aren't you?'

'You were doing a pretty good job of saving yourself when I saw you. Did they tell you you'd broken Jo's nose with your foot? Remind me never to get in your way in bed.'

She smiled a wan smile of resignation. 'I think we both know there's not much chance of that happening.'

A pause followed her words; she wasn't sure what she was expecting to come, and she wasn't sure whether she was more relieved or surprised when he did speak. 'It's my fault. I should have suspected how dangerous Jo was when we discovered he was stealing. I should have known he'd come after you.'

So he wasn't mourning her loss from his bed? That was good, wasn't it? Sophie's teeth found her lip, bit down on the pain of swollen tissue and suddenly realised the old habit was something she hadn't done for what seemed like ages.

She nodded numbly, wondering more about the lip than anything else. Maybe because that seemed easier to deal with.

'I want to explain about Jo.'

'There's no need.'

'Believe me, there's every need. Will you hear me?'

She sat down on the bed. What choice did she have? Until the doctor came, it wasn't as though she was going anywhere. And it wasn't as though it was going to change anything. 'Okay, I'm listening.'

He took a deep breath and blew it out in a rush. 'After Emma's death I got home from Italy as soon as I could. I couldn't believe it. I blamed myself for not insisting she come with us, like we'd originally wanted. I was a mess. I wanted to break something—someone—Jake. He was lying critically injured in a coma and I wanted to go finish the job.'

Sophie lowered her lashes, aching inside for her brother, lying in hospital so close to death, and for the tortured man who'd just lost his fiancée.

'Jo stopped me. At least, I thought he stopped me. I credited him with saving me in those dark days, of saving me from myself. When we met a few years later, after he'd been in the army and was looking for a job, I wanted to repay him. My business was just taking off. I gave him work, thinking I was repaying his friendship. His *loyalty*.'

He ground the word out between his teeth, his voice growing bitter. 'But all the time he was living a lie. I thought it bad enough when I discovered he was planning on pocketing half the pay-off money, but he'd already betrayed me in the worst possible way and I'd been too blind to see any of it. He told me that Jake had taken advantage of Emma while I was away and that he was probably taking her off for a back-street abortion to hide the evidence when they crashed. He fed me all this at the same time he was holding me back from wanting to tear your brother limb from limb.

'And to think I'd thanked him all these years for holding me back…' He shook his head. 'But then I learned of Monica's plans to marry Jake, and what had happened before all came rushing back. It wasn't just Jo feeding my hatred—I know I had more than plenty to go round myself—but it was almost as if Jo wanted your brother gone more. He told me your business was in trouble and needed cash. It all fitted with the idea your brother was in it for the money, and that you were too.'

He looked at her, his eyes dark with regret, underlined with shadows she hadn't noticed before. 'I was wrong, Sophie. So wrong.' He looked broken, shattered, and it was all she could do not to go to him, put her arms around him and tell him it didn't matter.

But it did matter. So many people's lives had been ruined back then; the shock waves continued to wreak devastation, even now, so she stayed where she was.

'It was Jo who got Emma pregnant,' she whispered. 'Not Jake. He… He raped her.'

And he closed his eyes, his chest expanding on a breath. 'I know. Which is why he didn't want Jake around.'

'But Jake couldn't remember.'

'Jo didn't know what he knew. He couldn't take the risk of the marriage going ahead and the truth coming out. He didn't want your brother anywhere near me. He was going to take the money and run. And he would have, if you hadn't tipped me off with numbers that didn't make sense. I have a lot to thank you for, Sophie. Even more to apologise for.'

It was something, at least.

'Jake seems to think Emma had come to him out of desperation. But I keep wondering why she didn't go straight to the police.'

'I don't know. Except her parents were very strict. Maybe she thought they wouldn't believe her. After all, he was supposed to be my friend. I'd asked him to look after her while I was away…'

She squeezed her eyes shut, wishing she could turn off his pain when she had so much of her own to bear. Because, if he'd blamed himself for her death before, now he had more reason than ever. Damn. She would not feel sorry for him! Not when he was hardly the victim in all this. She swallowed back on a sob.

'It was you who gazumped us at the Tropical Palms, wasn't it? So you could get me to the island. Have us all thinking the wedding was going ahead. All while you hatched your plan to pay off Jake in the background.'

His hands curled into fists at his sides. Then he nodded, his eyes the bleakest black.

'You made the phone call before the helicopter like I said, didn't you? And then you made out you'd been calling up the island, to let them know we were coming. You lied to me.'

'By omission—I tried to justify it to myself. But, yes, you're right. I lied to you.'

'And you were going to keep me, weren't you, as long as Jake had Monica? "An eye for an eye, a root for a root". That's how Jo put it. That's why you slept with me, wasn't it, Daniel? To get even at the basest level with someone you decided long ago you'd hate for ever.'

'Those were not my words!'

'But that was your intent! I was to be your prisoner in paradise, and you thought you might as well take advantage while I was here.'

'Sophie, it wasn't always like that, you have to believe me. Yes, I thought there was justice in having you with me while he had Monica. And, yes, to make that happen I made sure the Tropical Palms got an offer it couldn't refuse. I know that nobody can understand, but I had to do whatever I could to ensure I had complete control over this wedding. It was the only way. Only then, when you got here, I found more reason than ever for you to stay.'

'Because you had sex on tap?'

He blinked slowly and when he opened his eyes their deep sincerity almost made her look away. 'I told you you were the best, and it's true.'

She heard the rattle of a tea trolley and looked hopefully towards the door. Any interruption would be preferable right now to hearing these pointless words. She was good at sex, and he was in love with a dead woman.

It was never going to be a fair contest.

She stood up and started fussing with the recalcitrant zip on her bag, realised her toiletries were still in the bathroom and got frustrated with the slow progress. Where the hell was that doctor, anyway? Not that any doctor could help her now, because no doctor could help what was hurting inside her.

She took a calming breath. 'Look, Daniel, thanks for being there yesterday. Thanks for stopping by and explaining all that. Please give my regards to Millie. Please let her know I was relieved to hear she hadn't been hurt.'

He frowned. 'Where are you going?'

'Back to Brisbane. I have a flight booked. Meg's going to meet me at the airport.' She injected a dose of enthusiasm she didn't feel into her voice. 'I can't wait to catch up with all the news.'

'Sophie, I want you to come home.'

'I am going home, Daniel. My home.'

'But the wedding? What about the wedding?'

'Didn't you hear the news? I'm not needed here any more.'

He looked at her, dumbfounded. 'What are you talking about?'

'Why so shocked, Daniel? I thought you'd be pleased. It's what you wanted, after all: the wedding's off.'

His mind and senses reeled. He'd assumed he'd pick her up from the hospital and take her back to the island where he could soothe away her bruises, gentle her pain. He'd thought if he explained everything she might eventually understand, might forgive him.

She had to forgive him.

And he'd thought there was time, because there was a wedding to plan and she'd never walk away from that.

But if there was no wedding…

'What happened?'

She put a hand to her hip and tilted her head with the falsest smile she could muster. 'You know, it was the strangest thing. Apparently Monica overheard Jake talking to me on the phone and insisted he tell her what all the secrecy was about. When he told her that you were offering him money to break off the engagement, and had been responsible for dispensing with her last few boyfriends, she refused to believe you were capable of such a thing. You. The perfect brother.' She laughed a little. 'Imagine that.'

His hands fisted in his hair. What the hell had he done?

'So you'll no doubt be delighted to hear that they had a huge argument and it all got too hard—she couldn't marry anyone who didn't think the sun shone out of her brother, like she did, and he couldn't marry anyone who didn't believe him.'

She sucked in air.

'So you finally got what you wanted. I hope you're satisfied.'

She turned back toward her bags and made another effort at zipping up the zip, trying to make this chapter in her life final, all her efforts concentrated on the task in hand.

'Sophie—'

She spun back round. 'You're still here?'

'I'll speak to them. I'll fix it.'

'Good luck. It didn't sound too fixable when I heard the news.'

'You can't go. I said you were the best, Sophie. I meant it.'

Her sore lip suffered another ill-timed bite. 'You played me for a fool—making love to me and flattering me like you actually cared. When all the time you just wanted to keep me held hostage in paradise, so I'd fall for your charms and believe you took this wedding seriously. Why the hell shouldn't I go?'

'Because I love you.'

He wasn't sure who was the most shocked. She stood stock-still, her face drained of colour on one side, the garish blue bruises on the other standing out all the more.

While he reeled inside from the thunderclap discovery. *He loved her.* That was why he'd rejoiced when he'd discovered she wasn't after his money. That was why he'd rejoiced every time Jake had turned his offers down, and why he didn't rejoice when he'd heard the news the wedding was off. And that was why he'd never wanted to let her go.

'I didn't realise it myself. I didn't know until now. But why else would I spend hours in meetings thinking about you rather than what's on the agenda? Why would I rush home every day? Because I couldn't get you out of my head. I wanted to be with you, Sophie, because I love you.'

'No. You're in love with Emma. Always have been. Always will be.'

'I *loved* Emma. I know she'll always be special in my heart. But you're the one I love.'

She dipped her head in her hand and breathed deep. 'There are too many people hurting, Daniel. So much damage done. How can you expect me to embrace your love? How can you expect me to return it? Even… Even if I wanted to.'

She looked up to see hope in his eyes for the first time in days. 'Daniel, you have to let me walk away. You have to give me time.'

The door burst open, the doctor bustling in and swiping up the charts at the end of her bed near her packed bag. 'Someone anxious to go home, then?' He looked up at her, switched his glance to Daniel and turned his gaze down to the chart. 'Hope I didn't just interrupt something important.'

She gave a wan smile and shook her head. 'Not at all. Mr Caruana was just leaving.'

EPILOGUE

IT WAS the kind of day you wished you could bottle—not a cloud in the azure sky, the cerulean sea dotted with pleasure craft and a tempering sea breeze to keep the temperature from climbing too high.

It would have been perfect if her heart hadn't been permanently lodged in her mouth since she'd arrived.

Kallista had turned on its best and Meg had done a brilliant job bringing it all together while Sophie had held the fort in Brisbane these past couple of weeks. A white pavilion had been installed on a grassy patch near the shore and festooned with colourful bougainvillea over fluttering white chiffon, the perfect, romantic setting for the perfect wedding.

And it was. She'd slipped in, arriving on the very last launch when everyone was busy with last-minute details. She'd planned it that way. Even a couple of weeks away hadn't been enough to make her forget or stop her longing. But it seemed it had been long enough for Daniel. He hadn't contacted her in all that time. Clearly his profession of love hadn't meant a thing. She'd done the right thing by walking away.

What she hadn't planned was how highly strung she felt. She almost cried when she saw Jake up front with the celebrant, pulling at his collar, looking nervous and excited, like every proper groom should. She did cry when she saw

Monica, the most beautiful bride she'd ever seen, her smile joyous, her face radiant, as she walked down the aisle on the arm of her proud and equally beautiful brother to the man she loved.

The tears continued when she saw the men shake hands as one man handed the bride over to the other, and then when bride and groom exchanged vows and kissed she cried again.

She dabbed at her eyes as the congregation cheered the newly married couple and filtered behind them along the shore. At this rate she'd be a complete puddle by the time they made it to the speeches.

'It's good to see you again.'

She blinked and he was there, gloriously there before her, all magnificent male, dressed in a suit fit for a god. Appropriate, really, given what lay beneath. 'How have you been?'

Lonely.

'Busy. How about you?'

'The same.' He was looking at her with those hungry eyes, warm and sensual, his mouth turned into the beginnings of a smile although there were lines of strain there too. 'You look beautiful.'

She smiled. She had red eyes and a heavy heart, but she'd take the words in the spirit they were given.

'Sit with me at the reception,' he said. 'I got Meg to save you a seat.'

'Of course.' Sitting with him meant nothing. As sister of the groom, she'd expected not to be able to fade entirely into the woodwork. She could last a few hours in his company; she'd almost convinced herself.

They got corralled into wedding photos of family and friends and it seemed like ages before the party moved to the long-house pavilion. In pride of place was the cake Millie had made for them spilling with orchids in soft pinks and whites. 'It's beautiful, Millie,' she told the woman as they embraced. 'You've done a wonderful job.'

Millie wiped a tear from her own eye. 'We've missed you, Sophie. Him more than anyone. He's been like a bear with a sore head. Worse these last few days, waiting for you to turn up. You'd think he was the one getting married. Will you be staying a while?'

She smiled, not sure how she should feel about Millie's revelations. Excited? Hopeful? Or had he merely been dreading her presence. 'Just overnight. I have to be back in Brisbane.'

The older woman's face dropped momentarily. Then she sighed and nodded. 'I understand.'

Did she? Sophie wasn't sure she understood herself.

Finally everyone filed in and took their seats for the reception. Daniel held out her chair for her. He leaned down as she lowered herself, his warm breath like a living thing stroking her ear. 'I've missed you, Sophie.' And she felt his words all the way to her toes. 'I've missed you bad.'

'You didn't call.' She tried to keep the hurt from her voice, and failed miserably.

'I thought you needed space.'

'Oh.' What did that mean? But she nodded and picked up her wine, taking a sip, her eyes on the bride and groom. They were so happy and so much in love it almost hurt to look at them. 'How did you do it?' she asked. 'How did you get them back together again?'

He followed her gaze. 'I had a lot of bridges to mend before that happened. Luckily you'd shown me how.'

'I did? How?'

He looked around at the appetiser that had just been placed in front of them. 'Are you hungry?'

She shook her head. She knew what was on the menu; she'd put the courses together that week she'd spent on the island. She knew it would be fabulous without tasting a thing. Besides, there was something she needed more than food right now.

He took her hand and they headed for the beach, where the sun was just beginning to set, lighting the warm, tropical world with its soft glow.

'I spent too long in a world of hatred,' he said as they kicked off their shoes and set off along the sand. 'It consumed me. Powered me. Drove me to think I was doing right, when I was doing wrong. I hurt Monica. I thought I was protecting her and I hurt her.'

He stopped and looked at the sun and she saw the glint of moisture in the corner of his eyes. 'You taught me that the bonds of love were stronger than the chains of hate. You taught me that love wasn't about control. Love was being able to let something go, and trust you would keep it for ever.'

He looked down at her, taking her chin so softly in his fingers that her skin tingled at the contact. 'You taught me that, Sophie.

'And, even though I didn't want to let you walk away from me that day in the hospital, even though I knew it would break me and that however long it took would be hell, I knew in my heart that if I was ever to truly have you I would have to let you go and hope above hope that you would return to me.' He rested his forehead against hers and she put a hand to his cheek, relishing the touch of the face she had dreamed about every night since she'd left.

'Oh, Daniel.'

'So now… So now I need to know. Is there any chance for us, do you think? Is there any chance—after all the wrongs I've committed, after the nightmare I've put everyone through— that you might return to me and return my love?'

Her heart was singing so loud it was a wonder he couldn't hear its song of joy himself. 'I thought…I feared…'

'You thought what?'

'That you'd changed your mind. Realised that you'd made a mistake. I don't know. I just worried, when I hadn't heard from you, that I'd imagined you ever telling me.'

He put his arms around her. 'Not a chance. I haven't thought of anything else these last few weeks but how much I do love you. Marry me, Sophie. Marry me and make me the happiest man on earth.'

And suddenly there were more tears to contend with. Tears of joy, tears of relief, tears that welled up from a heart that swelled with love for him and washed away all the pain. 'Daniel, I love you so much!'

He pulled her, spinning, into his embrace and kissed her until she was dazed and drugged with the taste of him. Then he stopped spinning and dropped her feet to the sand. 'So you'll marry me?'

She smiled up at him, loving him, knowing she would love him for ever, knowing this tiny thing was not too much to ask. She pulled his head down and whispered in his ear and he smiled before pulling her back into another kiss.

It was late by the time they made it back to the reception; the cake had already been cut. They hung around the back of the pavilion so as not to interrupt, but Millie saw them entering, Sophie's hand encased in Daniel's, the sprig of bougainvillea he'd picked and woven into her hair, and she beamed and skirted around the tables towards them.

'It's the most magical wedding,' she said, taking in their knotted hands and the flush to their skin, her generous eyes both curious and hopeful. 'Just magical.'

'It's what Sophie's business promises,' Daniel grinned. 'One Perfect Day, to make perfect memories to last a lifetime,' and Sophie laughed.

'You memorised our advertising slogan!'

'I thought I might need it one day, if I ever needed a wedding planner.' He curled his arm around her and pulled her in tight. 'Turns out I might.'

Millie clapped her hands over her mouth. 'Oh lord, is it true?'

Sophie hugged the older woman. 'Daniel's asked me to marry him.'

Millie whooped with joy. 'And you said yes?'

'I told him I'd like to, but I want to make sure someone else gives their blessing too.' And she looked around, to find Daniel already threading his way through the crowd until he found his target. She watched him slap her brother on the back, she watched her brother frown as Daniel leaned close and then she saw his look of surprise as he sought her out, his frown transformed into a broad smile the second he saw her face and realised it was what she wanted.

She squeezed the older woman's hand. 'I think you better not hang those cake pans up in a hurry, Millie.'

Millie whooped again and hurried off to share the good news, not that Sophie was alone for long. Daniel was back and he picked her up and spun her around in his arms until she was dizzy. 'Thank you,' he said. 'How did you know that would feel so good? I feel like it's over. It's finally over.'

She laughed as he lowered her feet to the floor, dizzy with happiness as she cupped his face with her hands and held his gaze. 'No, Daniel. The way I prefer to think of it, it's only just beginning.'

His smile widened, his eyes radiating love. 'I like the way you think, Sophie Turner.'

And she feigned disappointment. 'Oh, and there was me thinking you liked the way I did something else.'

He growled his appreciation. 'Oh yes. I like that too. I like that a lot.' He looked around, suddenly agitated, that look back in his eyes. 'Is it too early to leave the party, do you think? It is my sister and your brother getting married, after all.'

She smiled up at him on a shrug and tugged on his hand. 'Sometimes you just have to be prepared to let go. Are you prepared to let go, Daniel?'

'Every night of my life.'

And she smiled and pulled him into the night. 'Then I'll keep coming back. For ever.'

'For ever,' he echoed as he swept her up into his kiss.

MILLS & BOON®

are proud to present our...

Book of the Month

The Baby Gift
A beautiful linked duet
by Alison Roberts from
Mills & Boon® Medical™

WISHING FOR A MIRACLE
Mac MacCulloch and Julia Bennett make the perfect
team. But Julia knows she must protect her heart –
especially as she can't have children. She's stopped
wishing for a miracle, but Mac's wish is standing right in
front of him – Julia...and whatever the future may hold.

THE MARRY-ME WISH
Paediatric surgeon Anne Bennett is carrying her sister's
twins for her when she bumps into ex-love Dr David
Earnshaw! When the babies are born, learning to live
without them is harder than Anne ever expected – and
she discovers that she needs David more than ever...

Mills & Boon® Medical™
Available 6th August

Something to say about our
Book of the Month?
Tell us what you think!
millsandboon.co.uk/community

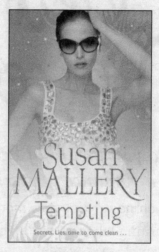

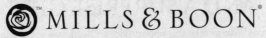

2 FREE BOOKS
AND A SURPRISE GIFT

We would like to take this opportunity to thank you for reading this Mills & Boon® book by offering you the chance to take TWO more specially selected books from the Modern™ series absolutely FREE! We're also making this offer to introduce you to the benefits of the Mills & Boon® Book Club™—

- **FREE home delivery**
- **FREE gifts and competitions**
- **FREE monthly Newsletter**
- **Exclusive Mills & Boon Book Club offers**
- **Books available before they're in the shops**

Accepting these FREE books and gift places you under no obligation to buy, you may cancel at any time, even after receiving your free books. Simply complete your details below and return the entire page to the address below. You don't even need a stamp!

YES Please send me 2 free Modern books and a surprise gift. I understand that unless you hear from me, I will receive 4 superb new books every month for just £3.19 each, postage and packing free. I am under no obligation to purchase any books and may cancel my subscription at any time. The free books and gift will be mine to keep in any case.

Ms/Mrs/Miss/Mr _____ Initials _____

_____

Surname _____

Address _____

_____

_____ Postcode _____

E-mail _____

Send this whole page to: Mills & Boon Book Club, Free Book Offer, FREEPOST NAT 10298, Richmond, TW9 1BR

Offer valid in UK only and is not available to current Mills & Boon Book Club subscribers to this series. Overseas and Eire please write for details.. We reserve the right to refuse an application and applicants must be aged 18 years or over. Only one application per household. Terms and prices subject to change without notice. Offer expires 31st October 2010. As a result of this application, you may receive offers from Harlequin Mills & Boon and other carefully selected companies. If you would prefer not to share in this opportunity please write to The Data Manager, PO Box 676, Richmond, TW9 1WU.

Mills & Boon® is a registered trademark owned by Harlequin Mills & Boon Limited. Modern™ is being used as a trademark. The Mills & Boon® Book Club™ is being used as a trademark.